FIREBRAT

FIREBRAT

by NANCY WILLARD

Illustrations by David Wiesner

ALFRED A. KNOPF · NEW YORK

THIS IS A BORZOI BOOK PUBLISHED BY ALFRED A. KNOPF, INC.

A Lucas/Evans Book

Manufactured in the United States of America
Designed by Mina Greenstein   10 9 8 7 6 5 4 3 2 1

Library of Congress Cataloging-in-Publication Data
Willard, Nancy. Firebrat.
A Lucas/Evans book.
Summary: Riding on the New York City subway, Molly and Sean
exit into the Crystal Empire and join a giant tortoise on a mission
to save the empire from the Firebrat. [1. Fantasy. 2. New York
(N.Y.)—Fiction] I. Wiesner, David, ill. II. Title.
PZ7.W6553Fi 1988 [Fic] 87-31060
ISBN 0-394-89008-6   ISBN 0-394-99008-0 (lib. bdg.)

TO BARBARA LUCAS,
my editor for eight books,
who showed me a picture by
David Wiesner and said,
"Write the story!"
I give this book
instead of flowers.

FIREBRAT

Knock, knock, knock.

"Molly," said her dad's voice, "you have to eat. Unlock the door immediately."

Molly unlocked the door but sat on her bed and would not look at him.

"It will only be for a month, Molly."

"Why me?" she wailed, forgetting her vow of silence. "Why not Betty? She's older."

"Because I think you'll do a better job than Betty. You're the reader in this family. The storyteller. Seems like I'm always picking up the phone and hearing how this kid or that kid wants Molly to come over and baby-sit because she tells such great stories."

Silence.

"Well, for heaven's sake, say something!"

I won't, she thought. I *can't*. If I open my mouth, I'll start bawling.

For months she'd looked forward to the last day of school and planned how she would spend the long summer afternoons. With Betty gone for vacation, Molly could have the house to herself. And she wouldn't have to hear Betty telling her to straighten up this and pick up that. She'd get up late, run a comb through her straight brown hair, and read or watch TV.

"Your grandma's getting awfully forgetful, Molly. Ever since Grandpa died, she's been living in the past—she tells the same stories over and over. She needs someone who'll talk to her and help her organize the shop. You know—keep her in touch with the present."

Silence.

"Molly, you're the one who doesn't mind a little mess." He waved his hand at her room. "You're the lover of mysteries."

"What's the big mystery about taking care of Grandma?"

"Making people well is always a mystery," said her father sadly.

He turned and closed the door behind him.

The next day Molly's mother took her shopping. New shoes, new jeans, two new dresses, a new purse. She's trying to buy me off, thought Molly.

That night, after she'd jammed her new clothes into the suitcase and her mother had made her take everything out and repack it, Molly had to admit it might be nice to get away from them all for a while.

Her dad lifted the suitcase and groaned.

"Don't take so many books. There's a library in New York."

"Take a cab to Grandma's apartment," said her mother. "And don't forget to tip the driver."

"I'll send you a postcard from Bermuda," said Betty.

For a whole month I won't have them lording it over me, Molly thought.

But the following morning when the train was pulling out and she didn't recognize a single face around her, and through the dirty window she saw Betty waving and her mother blowing her nose and her father making the victory sign with his fingers, Molly felt she was going to cry and wished the train would leave before the tears came. She felt inside her new purse—hideous black leather, not the little beaded one she'd liked that cost twice as much—and found a piece of packing paper at the bottom.

She'd forgotten the Kleenex.

"This is it," said the cab driver, and parked in front of the old brownstone, which looked so much like the houses on either side of it that Molly would not have picked it for her grandmother's if she hadn't seen the sign with the silver streetcar pointing to the shop in the basement.

THE SILVER SHUTTLE:
OLD AND NEW, NEAR AND FAR

Taped to the window was a small handwritten notice:

OPEN BY APPOINTMENT

The only person in sight was a boy on the front steps who looked to be about twelve. He wore a T-shirt that said DON'T TAKE LIFE SERIOUSLY, IT'S NOT PERMANENT, and he was trying to juggle with two bananas and an apple. When he dropped them, he consulted a book he kept open on his knees and tried again.

Molly paid the driver, tugged her suitcase out of the cab, and hauled it up the front steps, past the boy, into the foyer.

She tried the door. Locked. The boy had stopped juggling to watch her.

"You have to ring the bell," he said.

"I *know*," said Molly. "I've been here before."

Inspecting the wall of buzzers with names neatly printed beside them, she found her grandmother's name.

E. WALLACE

She pushed the buzzer. When nobody came, she leaned on it.

"Mrs. Wallace went out with the woman who comes every day," said the boy. "Who are you?"

"I'm Molly. I'm her granddaughter."

"I'm Sean. Your grandmother might not be back for ages and ages," said the boy. "You can wait in our place if you want to. We live across the hall."

Together they pushed Molly's suitcase ahead of them, and Sean unlocked the door to number seven. What a wonderful place to roller skate! thought Molly as she stepped into a single corridor with rooms opening off to the right. You could look into all of them.

"We just moved here two months ago," said the boy.

He paused before a room that was even neater than Betty's. The shelves on the bookcase were meticulously labeled:

COMICS	SAMURAI BOOKS
SCIENCE FICTION	*MAD* MAGAZINES
COINS	CARTOON BOOKS
KARATE BOOKS	WORLD WAR II STUFF

Under the bookcase rested two barbells. Molly searched for the right thing to say.

"You sure have a lot of comics. Why are they all in plastic bags?"

"I have a very valuable collection. I have almost a complete run of 'Iron Man.' "

"My mother never lets me buy comics," said Molly.

"Too bad," said Sean. " 'Iron Man' is great. But 'Swamp Thing' is my favorite. Anything I want, my mom buys it for me."

The curtain waving over the open window was covered with buttons: DOCTOR WHO, STAR EXPLORER/HAYDEN PLANETARIUM, 1983 CHAMPION PHILLIES, I READ BANNED BOOKS, I ♥ CALIFORNIA.

"California," sighed Molly. "I'd love to live in California."

"My dad sent that one. I visit him every summer."

"Neat," said Molly.

"No, it's awful. He always wants to go rock climbing. He has this thing about conquering peaks. And he always signs me up for Little League. I hate it. And he wants me to make the All-Stars. Just because he won a bronze medal for track in the Olympics when he was in college."

He pointed to a cigar box on the bureau. "Help yourself to a subway token."

Molly lifted the lid of the box.

"You must have hundreds of them! Where did you get so many?"

"Eugene brings them," said Sean. "You should see the stuff he brings to the shop. All kinds of neat junk. He finds it in the subway."

"Who's Eugene?" asked Molly.

"He's—he's just Eugene," said Sean. "I think he used to be a sailor before he started living in the subway."

"He *lives* in the subway?"

"He says he lives in the subway."

"That's terrible," said Molly.

"But sometimes he says he doesn't," said Sean. "And he's got this wonderful silver ring. It's got a glass eye, and he's going to give it to me someday."

Suddenly they caught the sound of voices and a distant door being unlocked.

"Your grandma is home," he said. "I hope you come back tomorrow."

The door to her grandmother's apartment stood open, and a large woman in a black dress and a baggy blue cardigan was coming to close it. When she spied Molly dragging her suitcase, she threw up her hands.

"You must be Molly. Edna! Edna!"

The room into which she led Molly was crammed with overstuffed furniture. The chairs wore doilies crocheted in green and lavender and gold on their arms. And photographs were everywhere, stuck in cheap frames and propped on the table or taped to the walls: snapshots of Grandma and Grandpa in Florida, of Betty and Molly blowing out the candles on their birthday cakes, of Betty diving, of Molly dressed as Scrooge for the school play two years before. Piles of magazines and newspapers rose in neat columns against one wall, and every table, every bookcase, was crammed with knickknacks, colored glass bottles, and salt and pepper shakers.

Grandma was lying on the sofa. She was plumper than Molly remembered her, but she still had the same red wavy hair that fluffed around her face. Once Molly had asked Grandma why she never had any gray hair, and Grandma had answered, "The secret is Loving Care, my dear, Loving Care." Betty, who knew everything worth knowing about beauty secrets, told her Loving Care was a rinse that covered up the gray. You could buy Loving Care in the drugstore.

"You're late," said Grandma, and slowly, very slowly,

she stood up and gave Molly a hug. "Alice, I thought you said she was coming yesterday."

"Now, Edna, you know she wasn't supposed to come till today. Let's show Molly her room."

I hope it's not all jammed up like this one, thought Molly.

The instant Molly entered the room, which adjoined her grandmother's, she wanted to weep. Before her she saw a cot, with the sheets and blankets stacked neatly on the pillow, an old bureau, a vacuum cleaner, and a wrought-iron floor lamp in the shape of an alligator.

"I picked this lamp especially for you, Molly," remarked Grandma. "I want it out by ten o'clock each night. In its prime, this lamp was lovely."

"Lovely," echoed Alice.

Horrible, thought Molly. She would call her parents tonight. Surely they would let her come home when she told them about the room.

"Eugene brought it," continued Grandma.

"I don't trust Eugene," said Alice. "Imagine, a grown man living in the subway on KitKats and pizza."

"I saw him eating an apple once," said Grandma. "And he can fix anything. He can even shoe horses."

"What kind of man would hang around subways?"

"He's perfectly honest," said Grandma.

Alice did not look convinced.

"He tried to steal the doorknob off Mrs. O'Brien's apartment."

"He was only borrowing it," said Grandma. "He brought her a much prettier one. White china, with roses on it." She stared long and hard at Molly and announced, "Molly is hungry."

"I put two TV dinners in the oven," said Alice. "I'll show her where the silverware is, so she can set the table."

"She can bring the TV to the table," said Grandma. "I don't want to miss my nature program."

They talk about me just as if I weren't here, thought Molly. I should be so lucky.

When Alice was gone, Molly opened the oven door and peeked under the foil.

Fish and spinach. Yuk.

The TV was chattering away in Grandma's room. Molly fled to her own room, slammed the door, and threw herself on the bed. Just like camp, she thought. Make your own bed. Lights out at ten.

She unsnapped her suitcase and dumped her clothes on the floor. Tears running down her face, she opened the top drawer of the bureau to put her things away and found it was crammed with snapshots and empty medicine bottles.

Grandma didn't leave me any space.

Angrily she yanked out a handful of snapshots. What she saw in the top photograph took her breath away. A girl her own age who had Molly's face was standing in front of a barn with a large snake in her hands, smiling. She wore a

middy blouse and a long skirt and high-buttoned shoes. Molly turned the picture over and read the name scrawled on the back:

Edna Hester, 12

It was at that moment Molly smelled something burning and heard Grandma shouting, "The dinner! The dinner!"

In the smoky living room Molly and her grandmother ate burned fish and spinach, Molly choking on hers, her grandmother eating with real pleasure. On the TV screen flickered sinister pictures of mushrooms and mold.

I'm going to throw up, Molly said to herself, and thought how awful it would be to clean it up afterward.

"I love fungi," said Grandma. "Lots of mushrooms grew in the woods behind our house when I was a girl. I knew them all by name."

Molly shuddered. Before her lay a whole evening with Grandma. A whole evening of watching mushrooms on TV.

By ten o'clock Grandma was snoring in her chair. Molly turned off the TV. She was too tired to make up her bed. She lay down and fell asleep in her clothes and never opened her eyes till the next morning, when she saw Grandma standing at the foot of the cot.

"I thought you'd never wake up. It's nearly ten o'clock!" Grandma exclaimed.

"Is Alice here?" asked Molly. She still felt tired. She hoped she wouldn't have to spend every waking minute with her grandmother.

"Alice won't be coming so often, now that I have you. If you want to fix up your room, run on down to the shop. You'll find a lot of real nice stuff there."

I'll bet, thought Molly.

"Sean can show you around. He looks just like Timothy Bean."

"Who is Timothy Bean?" asked Molly.

"You wouldn't know him. I had a crush on him in sixth grade. He gave me a little gold heart, and I promptly lost it. He's probably dead and gone now."

And she handed Molly a large brass key.

Grandma hovered over her while she sat at the kitchen counter and ate a cold English muffin. Molly looked hopefully around for juice and cereal but saw none.

"I wish I could remember Sean's last name," said Grandma. "I used to know it." She gave Molly an anxious look. "I can't remember a thing anymore. I might just as well die."

A feeling of helplessness washed over Molly. She stepped into the hall and bumped into Sean, who glanced at the key in her hand and smiled.

"Are you going down to the shop?" he asked eagerly. "I've got my flashlight."

The CLOSED TODAY sign crashed to the floor when Molly
unlocked the door, and they entered the cold, dark shop.
Sean turned on the overhead light, which cast a dim pallor
over the center of the room. Never had Molly seen a room
so crammed with curiosities. Behind a broken rose arbor,
stacks of chairs towered over a traffic jam of sofas. Under
the glass top of a broad counter glittered cameos, earrings,
crosses, and spoons, all presided over by a large porcelain
head engraved with a map of the brain. Molly did not want
to touch anything for fear of spiders. The darkness and the
silence unnerved her.

"It feels like somebody's hiding here," she whispered.

Sean beamed the light first on a box of moth crystals,
then on a stuffed kid glove loaded with rings. It rose like a
ghostly hand over the counter, as if inviting them to
inspect the boxes of buttons and jars of sea shells and piles

of old records and a birdcage that wore a little sign: BROKEN—BIRD WON'T SING. From the bars dangled a torn Dracula mask with a Woolworth's price tag in its mouth, as if it were sticking out its tongue at the cabinet full of trophies, in which half a dozen tiny golden men with drawn pistols stood on pedestals engraved FIRST PRIZE. The names of the winners had disappeared.

Sean opened the cabinet and fingered a trophy.

"I could take one of these and tell my dad I won it," he said. "Eugene would give me one. I wish I had a trophy of my own. Or at least a medal."

A sign that said WALK-IN DOCTOR, MAN OR BEAST was leaning against a pile of old books. Hoping for a good mystery story, Molly pulled one out, bound in faded calico.

How to Fix Everything!
Hints for the Busy Housewife

She flipped through it, skimming the subject headings: "Comforters." "Moths." "Rhinestones." "Silverfish." All at once something that looked like a scorpion with too many legs sprang to the floor and scuttled away. Shrieking, Molly dropped the book. Sean laughed.

"That's nothing but a firebrat. Don't you have them where you live?"

"No," said Molly, shuddering.

"Mostly they stay under the radiators," said Sean.

"What I really hate are the cockroaches. Everybody in New York has cockroaches. Do you see anything here you want?"

What she wanted was her own room with its familiar disorder and the smell of supper downstairs and her mother asking if she'd picked up her clothes yet.

I've got to pull myself together, she said to herself.

She saw nothing she wanted except two little golden fish in the jewelry case. Shining softly on their golden chains, they might have been caught in far-off waters. The case was not locked. Molly lifted the glass and took out a fish.

"Oh, I want that!" exclaimed Sean.

"There's one for each of us," said Molly.

When she slid the chain over her head, something crashed to the floor behind her, and a huge figure darkened the doorway, shuffling and shaking its antlered head and singing:

> *"The man in the ocean, he asked of me*
> *How many children live in the sea?*
> *I answered him as I thought good,*
> *As many fishes as live in the wood."*

Molly screamed.

"Eugene!" shouted Sean.

He was dressed like the captain of a ship, with gold stripes on his cuffs and an anchor on his sleeve and work gloves and a visored cap such as Greek fishermen wear in

the travel posters, and on his head he was carrying the head of a stuffed moose. When he set down the moose's head, his cap fell to the floor. His blue eyes looked straight through Molly.

"Don't be afraid, Molly!" he roared.

"How did you know my name?" asked Molly.

"Your grandma told me. And you look just like her. The moment I laid eyes on you, I said to myself, 'Who else could this be but Molly!'"

"I don't look like Grandma," said Molly. "She's old and I'm not."

"Have you never seen a picture of her when she was young?" asked Eugene. "You two could be sisters. Now, where's that music box your grandma wanted fixed? Is it that one?"

He opened the door of the birdcage, took out a little brass bird, and stuck it in his back pocket, and Molly caught a chilling glimpse of the ring he wore on his middle finger: a glass eye, as blue as the sea, set in a silver eyelid.

"Did you bring me a present, Eugene?" demanded Sean.

"I brought you a map," replied Eugene. "Don't thank me. But you might want to thank the subway. I found this map blowing down a tunnel under Canal Street. I keep my eye on things. I look for clues."

"What kind of clues?" asked Sean.

"I don't know till I find them," said Eugene. "Lost cities. Fish that swim in the air. I keep my eye on things. Did you drop this, Molly?"

With a sweep of his hand he scooped *How to Fix Everything!* from the floor and handed it to her.

"Thank you," said Molly nervously.

"Tell your grandma next time I come I'll bring her a strand of cultured pearls. Very cultured. They speak French and love classical music. Now, what would make a good trade?"

His glance darted around the shop and came to rest on the Dracula mask and the broken rose arbor.

"A fine mask," he said, and tucked it under his arm.

"But it's torn," objected Molly. "What are you going to do with it?"

"Give it to a friend," he replied. "He's a little bored, a little lonely. He needs a nice Dracula mask to take his mind off himself. . . ."

He hoisted the broken arbor over his head and staggered toward the door, singing:

> *"Fair trade, fair trade,*
> *A strand of pearls for a broken arbor,*
> *Fair trade, fair trade,*
> *I'm going uptown to the magic harbor."*

And out the door he marched.

Sean unfolded the map.

"It's only a subway map," he said. "But I'll keep it. Maybe it'll come in handy."

He folded the map and tucked it into his belt.

After a week Grandma declared she hadn't felt so well in years. Molly felt terrible. Afternoons Grandma would say, "Let's get out my box of snapshots and tell stories—we come from a long line of storytellers," just as if she hadn't looked at the same snapshots the afternoon before and told Molly the same stories. Best of all Grandma liked pictures of herself when she was Molly's age. She loved to talk about the one in which she and another girl were holding up a long, black snake. They were holding it between them like a clothesline, and smiling.

"That picture of me and my best friend was taken on the farm in Michigan," she'd say, just as if Molly didn't know, "and I wish I could remember where she moved when she grew up. Her name was Cora Dibble, and we sent each other Christmas cards for years. And one year she didn't put her return address on the envelope, and I just lost track of her. I'd love to see Cora Dibble again."

Molly nodded. She knew exactly what Grandma would say next.

"I love snakes—the nonpoisonous ones. Our dog brought this one home. I took it from his jaws and set it free. I'll bet that snake never forgot me. Your dad used to love for me to tell that story."

One day when Molly brought the box of snapshots, Grandma said, "Molly, I want you to have my rattlesnake ring. I've been saving it for you."

And she lifted her hand to show Molly a chain of tiny bone beads that circled the little finger of her left hand.

"Oh!" said Molly, horrified.

"I found it in the woods right after this picture was taken, and I always figured it was a present from the snakes."

"Oh, I couldn't take it," said Molly. "I'd probably lose it." It's gross, she thought. Really gross.

But Grandma had slipped the ring off her own finger and was holding it out to her.

"I'd be real glad to see you wearing this ring. Put it on."

Molly put it on. It was still warm from Grandma's hand.

If it hadn't been for Sean and Eugene, Molly was sure she'd go crazy. Every afternoon she and Sean went treasure hunting in the shop. Eugene would come by with a bag of bagel chips or glazed doughnuts from the bakery down the block and they'd pull up three chairs around an old card table, and Molly and Sean would watch new treasures appear from Eugene's shopping bag: an old toy fire engine with cast-iron horses and a tank to hold the water, or a box of five hundred doilies, each one different.

"I got them from a spider in exchange for a sewing machine," said Eugene.

One day he brought them a wooden frog inlaid with fake emeralds that was really a music box. It played "Raindrops Keep Falling on My Head" when you opened its mouth.

But best of all was the box of subway tokens Eugene kept in his pocket, for this led to the best trick of all.

"Where's that fix-it book, Molly?" he'd say. "Some evil genie broke my spell. How am I going to fix it?"

And while they were looking for the book, they'd forget to watch his hands, and he'd reach over and take a token from Molly's ear or Sean's sneaker. And the eye in his ring seemed to twinkle.

"When can I have that ring?" Sean asked one day. "You promised, Eugene."

"When you are as great a magician as I am."

"I can't be that! I don't know how to do your magic."

"In time, Sean, you may be a greater magician than I," Eugene assured him.

The subway map was still spread out on the card table, where Molly and Sean had been playing a game that Eugene said was the right thing to do with a subway map and two old checkers and a quarter. You flipped for moves, and whoever got from Van Cortlandt Park to South Ferry in the fewest moves won. They'd played for days, and Molly was tired of it now.

She glanced around for something to read, and *How to Fix Everything!* fell off the shelf, as if it had read her mind. Remembering that the firebrat had leaped out of the book the first time she noticed it, she picked it up cautiously and flipped through a chapter titled "Invisible Reweaving," which was followed by a chapter called "Noxious Insects." And there, to her delight, was a page headed FIREBRATS, with a picture and a description.

THE FIREBRAT
Thermobia domestica

The entry read:

Firebrats are nocturnal insects that can do a great deal of damage to paper and clothing. They like warm areas, the attic in summer, and the area of the furnace in winter.

Above the text a meticulously drawn firebrat lazed in the borders of the picture.

It looks like a crayfish with more legs than anything in this world ought to have, thought Molly. The word *silverfish* caught her eye. She had never heard of silverfish but they sounded beautiful. She tucked the book into her pocket just as the shop door banged open and Sean ran in.

"Sorry I'm late. I brought you a 7-Up."

"Thanks," she said. As she pulled the tab off the can it hissed and foamed, and a fine spray shot out and covered her, the floor, the table, the map. Sean burst out laughing.

"You've wrecked the game, dummy!" shouted Molly. "Get a towel!"

"Get it yourself!" Sean shouted back.

They were teetering on the edge of a quarrel when Molly glanced down and gave a cry of astonishment.

Something extraordinary was happening to the map. Behind the red and blue lines of the subway, another map was coming into focus. The artist had painted every tree, every bush, as if he were making a map for birds. And now a river appeared like a crack down the middle. To the left of the river the land was without detail, a flickering red, as if the artist had grown tired and hurried to finish. The names of the subway stations were fading. Only Garden Street shone through like a memory. To the left of the street was an iron grill, and in the middle of the grill glittered a golden carp, its tail pointing to the center of the map.

For several minutes Molly and Sean could only stare in amazement. It was Molly who broke the silence.

"Do you think this is a real place?"

Sean scratched his head.

"Garden Street is real," he said. "But there's no station there. I wish Eugene were here. Oh, Molly, let's get up early tomorrow morning and check it out!"

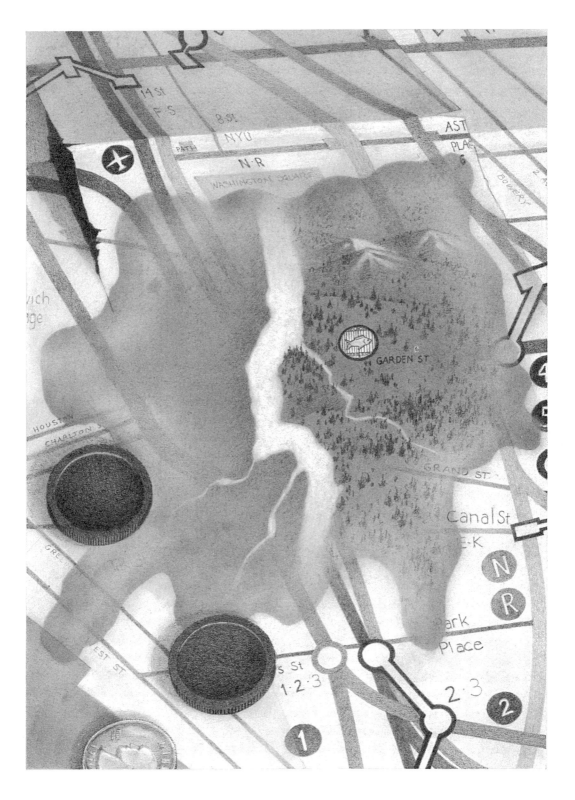

At eight o'clock the next morning, Sean was on the front steps waiting for her.

"Oh," he exclaimed. "You wore your fish too!"

Molly nodded.

"Did you bring the map?" she asked.

"What for? I don't need a map to get around the city. Open your hand."

From a pocketful of subway tokens he took five and dropped them into her open palm.

"Will we need so many?" asked Molly.

"I always carry extras, in case I lose one. You have to be prepared. I brought my flashlight, too."

All around them the city was waking up: awnings were pulled down and gates were pulled up from the windows of shops. Here a girl was setting out potted palms for sale, there a man was hanging a banner over a dozen brass bedsteads that gleamed in the sun: EVERYTHING MUST GO.

"We'll take the express," said Sean, and he darted across the street.

Two green globes glowed like peculiar planets on either side of the steps that led down, down. We're going right under the city, thought Molly, hurrying after him. A cool breeze folded around them; for an instant she felt as if she were flying into a cave of dark wind.

They turned the corner, dropped in their tokens, pushed through the turnstile, and joined half a dozen other people on the platform, all staring across the tracks at other platforms and beyond them other tracks. Nobody except Molly so much as glanced at the advertisements that blazoned on the walls around them. Under a huge roll of Kodak a slogan caught her attention like a shout: TIME GOES BY! Next to it a parrot as tall as Molly herself perched on the words CUERVO PREMIUM TEQUILA! ANYTHING CAN HAPPEN!

"Come on, Molly, let's—"

A train rushed past and its roar sucked up Sean's words. The newsstand, the turnstile, the benches, the people waiting—everything seemed about to be swept away.

Then the train was gone. The air stood so still Molly could hear water dripping. She was about to ask Sean if he heard it too when a second train rushed through the darkness toward them, beaming its light on the walls, as if searching for something—a face, a sign, a window—before it screeched to a stop.

Sean grabbed Molly's hand and pulled her onto the train.

"The seats are all taken," he told her. "Hang on to the pole."

How bright and exciting it all was! And everyone else was dozing or reading a paper. Nobody except Molly and Sean cared to look out the window at the names of the stations and the platforms lit like stages flashing past them while the wheels struck blue sparks from the tracks. Under the ad for missing children an elderly woman dozed. Molly studied the pictures: six children. Would I be able to recognize them if they were on this train? she thought. The pictures were probably taken a long time ago. Sean nudged her.

"I'd like to send that one to my dad," he said, pointing up at a poster of the New York skyline, over which floated the words THE ADVENTURE BEGINS IN YOUR OWN BACKYARD.

"Our stop is next," said Sean. "Get ready to move."

They stood at the door, pressing their faces to the glass. Suddenly the lights went out and the train slowed down.

And stopped.

"What's wrong?" asked Molly. By the faint glow of the emergency light over the door, she could just see Sean's profile.

"It always does this," said a man's voice behind them.

"I hope we're not stuck," said a woman's voice.

The voice of the conductor crackled through the loud-speaker.

"Mmms ssb bwwwwaw."

Really, thought Molly, he might just as well be speaking underwater.

Lights flickered, the train crept forward. Suddenly Sean grabbed her arm.

"Molly, look!"

Behind the reflection of their own faces in the window, they both saw it: a ghostly platform, caught in the head-light of a train passing in the opposite direction. Then it vanished into the darkness.

"That was it! That was Garden Street!" exclaimed Sean.

"But we can't reach it," said Molly.

"Yes, we can. There must be a way to get in. We only have to walk back a block."

The lights in the car flashed on, safe and familiar, and for a moment Molly hoped that they wouldn't find the way in.

By the time she'd climbed the steps to the street she was out of breath. She looked around in bewilderment at the bustle of shoppers jostling one another in the street. How different it was from her grandmother's street, with its quiet brownstones and apartment buildings. Here were fish stores, shoe stores, coffee shops, markets, taxis darting between buses and delivery trucks, horns honking, motors racing, the smell of exhaust. Three street signs pointed the way to the Holland Tunnel, as if it were easy to lose, or hard to find.

"Wouldn't that be something—a tunnel all the way to Holland?" Molly shouted. She could hardly keep up with Sean, who was jogging his way through the crowd. Suddenly he paused at a fire hydrant wearing a cap of painted stars and studied the street signs.

"It might be across the street, near that park," he said.

The park disappointed her. It was hardly more than an island where the streets came together. What might have been grass once was bricked over, and everything under the mottled sycamores looked dirty, as if a tide had washed up its cargo of plastic spoons, matches, cigarette butts, and torn papers. Four men in hard hats were sitting on one of the benches, drinking coffee from plastic cups. The pigeons that wheeled around them had sad, tarnished feathers, like old pewter.

Music was blaring from the open door of a record store:

> *"I'd like to be under the sea*
> *in an octopus's garden in the shade.*
> *He'd let us in, knows where we've been,*
> *in his octopus's garden in the shade."*

In the gutter, a smashed fender gleamed like a broken wing.

"It ought to be right here," muttered Sean.

"Over there, behind you—isn't that a subway station? It's got a green globe."

The wrought-iron rails and one of the globes were gone, and the other was partly smashed. Plastic garbage bags littered the steps, half hidden under the skeleton of an old Christmas tree from which stray shreds of tinsel still fluttered. But the stairs were not boarded up. Sean pushed the tree aside, and a voice said, "You dumb kids—that station's been closed for years."

One of the men on the bench laughed at them. No one else seemed to notice them.

"At least we can look through the grille," said Sean.

The iron gate was padlocked and chained.

Disappointed, Molly leaned forward and tried in vain to peer past it. As she did so the little golden carp swung from the chain at her throat and chimed against the lock—*ping, ping, ping.* The gate did not spring open, but seemed to shift and fade. When she stretched out her hands, she found no gate at all but bare branches. Pulling them apart, she stepped through to the other side.

Sean gave a shout of amazement. "How did you—"

"The fish, the fish! Tap your fish against the padlock!"

Holding the golden fish, Sean tapped once.

Ping.

"Try it again," urged Molly.

Ping, ping sang the fish against the lock, and the bars bent into branches which closed swiftly after him.

The stairs, the token booth, everything felt old and

down at the heels, or down on its luck. Molly's heart was pounding as she followed the beam of Sean's flashlight into darkness.

Then all at once he vanished. She heard footsteps running away from her.

"Where are you?" she shouted.

A train rumbled closer and closer.

"Molly, I've found it!"

By the light from the cars as the train flew past them she saw the turnstiles, the empty benches, and Sean dancing up and down and waving his flashlight at her.

Though the name of the station was long gone, the picture of a fish tiled right into the wall was not even cracked. The air smelled musty; the wooden turnstiles which once opened for a nickel—it said 5¢ under the slot— now spun free, and on the bench fluttered a poster that showed a submarine nosing the waves behind faded red, white, and blue letters:

LOOSE LIPS SINK SHIPS

"Hey, that's a World War Two submarine," exclaimed Sean. "This poster is really *old*—"

In his excitement he turned off the flashlight and plunged them into a darkness so total that Molly felt as if she had gone blind.

"Sean!"

Click. The friendly beam awoke.

"Sorry." Sean sounded a little shaken himself. "Wait till we tell Eugene!" he crowed. "What a great place to look for treasure. We can pretend it's King Tut's tomb. Let's see if we can find the other exit."

Molly shivered. They ran through the turnstile and Sean beamed his flashlight this way and that.

Sure enough, here was the other flight of stairs. The flashlight caught a flutter of dead leaves on the bottom step.

"I hear water dripping," said Molly.

"You can always hear water dripping in the subway," said Sean. He shone his light up the stairs. "It's probably boarded up."

They climbed the first five steps and saw a faint light at the top, which grew brighter and brighter as they climbed higher and higher, and now a fragrance of roses greeted them and the glad, fresh smell of a forest after rain, and Sean laid his flashlight on one of the steps; he did not need it anymore.

High overhead arched a canopy of trees.

The handrail was half hidden under dead brambles. Light sifting through the trees silvered the steps with broken stars, and the brambles gave way to a leafy vine that festooned the handrail and burst into roses at the top of the stairs.

"Oh!" cried Molly.

The stairway had led them into a forest so still they could hear themselves breathing. There were birches and beeches and sycamores and oaks, streaked with a pale light from the two gas lamps above the railing. And how broad the trees were! It seemed to Molly they must have been growing before time began. Their roots stretched and curled like sleepy animals. Clinging to their muscular backs and nestled in the rough ripples of bark stood row after row of cottages no bigger than Molly's hand.

Two large fish floated by, their tails undulating among the branches.

It was then Molly noticed the sidewalk, cracked and broken, which ended at their feet. Eugene's song popped into her head: *I answered him as I thought good, as many fishes as live in the wood.* Fish swimming through the air of a lost city.

"Look!" whispered Sean.

A giant tortoise was crunching the dead leaves and scuffling over the broken pavement, making its way toward them.

"You've come at last! If you'd sent word ahead of time, I would have ordered the lamps lit along the Great Jade Road all the way to the Perfect Emperor's palace. But it's too late now," said the tortoise in a rusty voice.

He was big enough to carry both Molly and Sean. Moss furred his shell with every shade of green, like a stone that has lain undisturbed for years, and his leathery toes made a dry, scraping sound on the broken squares of pavement, and when at last he stood before them, huffing and puffing, Molly noticed something flashing in the spots where the moss wore thin. A keyhole here, a hinge there.

"But you're very late, O Most Powerful Magicians from the Upper World," he scolded. "Five hundred years is a long time to wait."

"There must be some mistake," said Molly quickly. "We're not magicians."

The tortoise blinked.

"But you are exactly the way you were described to us. A wise man said, 'They will be young, and you shall know them by the golden fish they wear at their throats. And they will bring you the Book That Fixes Everything.'"

Molly shivered. Her knees felt as if they were turning to water. The tortoise did not notice.

"Since you've arrived without warning, O Most Powerful Magicians, the Perfect Emperor won't have had time to call out the tea things. The cups are probably all grown over with weeds, and the saucers are sleeping with the clams in the mud."

"Emperor?" exclaimed Sean. "What *is* this place?"

"You have arrived, of course, at what remains of the Crystal Empire. And I have orders to take you to the palace as soon as possible. Let us set out along the Great Jade Road at once. The emperor is waiting."

And he turned around the way he had come and began to pull himself along the pavement, treading carefully to avoid the brambles that pushed up between the cracks.

"Molly, let's follow him," whispered Sean, who very much liked being addressed as a most powerful magician. "We can always go back the way we came."

The tortoise overheard him and wagged his head.

"No, you can't. The gate you came in by can only be used to enter. To go back you must go through the Firebrat's kingdom."

Molly's heart sank.

"Who is the Firebrat?" asked Sean.

"Hush! Not so loud! Don't you know how dangerous he is? You've seen his picture in your ancient book. Who but the Firebrat could have lived in the Mountain of One Hundred Tempers? What other swordsmith tempers his blades in rage? Who but the Firebrat could make Killkeep?"

"Killkeep?" repeated Sean.

"A sword so merciless it would kill its master if it had the chance. And now you two have arrived to save the Crystal Empire of the Perfect Emperor."

"I'm sure there's been a mistake," said Molly. "I'm Molly and this is my friend Sean. We—"

"Please don't dawdle," interrupted the tortoise. "It's an arduous journey to the palace, but I shall have time to tell you why you find us in such a state of twilight."

Arduous for him or for us? thought Molly. She did not like arduous journeys. Surely the emperor could show them another way home. She shaded her eyes and looked eagerly ahead of them, but saw no palace—nothing but trees.

"The palace—where is it?" she asked.

"Children, once the palace was lovely," said the tortoise. "It was like a lantern in which the moon rises. Crystal pagodas glittered over jade roses, silver staircases lead to crystal gardens, leaf chimed on leaf, dragonflies hummed and thrummed. But the great attraction of our island was the crystal garden. First you came to the nursery, the little houses where each new crystal was started and grew till it could be transplanted into the main garden. These we were able to take with us from the island, though none of the crystals we brought are yet ripe."

"What island?" demanded Sean.

"The island which the Firebrat caused us to leave, of course. The Island of a Thousand Lights. Ah, children, our island was a jewel in the Sea of Forgetfulness. To the west rose the Mountain of One Hundred Tempers. Smoke hid the top of the mountain and no roads led there. To the east grew our timestick tree, the cause of all our grief."

"I've never heard of a timestick tree," said Molly.

The tortoise paused for breath.

"For every citizen on our island a timestick grew. It was picked at birth and brought to the Temple of Justice and lighted. The tree was closely guarded by two dragons, lest one of the timesticks should go out and take a life with it. Children, our timesticks burned for one hundred years, and near the end of that time we would grow sick and weak."

"How terrible!" exclaimed Molly. The palace was still nowhere to be seen. If there is a palace, it must be very far away, she thought. Was the tortoise lying to them?

"When the light on a timestick was almost gone, a person could go to the tree and light it again from a younger timestick and live a hundred years more. We had a lovely ceremony for the relighting of the timesticks. We sang, we danced, we gave gifts . . ."

"Go on about the tree and the dragons," said Sean.

"Don't hurry me," said the tortoise. "Where was I?"

"You were relighting the timesticks," said Sean.

"I was indeed," said the tortoise. "But the great attraction of our garden was not the timesticks. No, it was our crystals. Our crystals had the power to end all quarrels. They were called crystals of forgiveness, and emperors from other kingdoms traveled great distances for them. Every morning we threw a handful of crystals into the sea so that forgiveness might wash ashore in countries where it was needed most. For every crystal we sent out, the Firebrat sent three invisible swords to scatter sparks of hatred."

"I suppose the crystals cost a lot of money," said Sean, who was always interested in what things cost.

"We never took money for them," said the tortoise. "We traded them for gifts that would improve our island. It was one of these gifts that changed our lives forever."

And now Molly found herself listening attentively, in spite of herself.

"One day the emperor of Japan brought us three crickets in gold and silver cages. Our Perfect Emperor was very young, younger than yourself, sir, with no mother and father to advise him, for when he was sent to us from the Sea of Forgetfulness, he left all his memories behind him."

"Does your Perfect Emperor know any samurai?" asked Sean.

"I'm coming to that part," said the tortoise. "The emperor of Japan brought a gift of three crickets. 'My crickets look poor,' he said, 'but they are very clever.' He picked up the golden cage and whispered, 'Sing, Golden Bells.' Such a marvelous chirping and trilling answered him! As the cricket sang the Perfect Emperor remembered the stairways of light in his green jade pavilion under the waves of the Sea of Forgetfulness."

"What about the samurai?" demanded Sean.

"The emperor of Japan took the other two crickets out of the silver cage. They were suited like samurai, and they waved tiny swords. And the emperor of Japan said, 'Fight, Fire and Water, fight!' The two crickets charged at each other—*crick! crack!*—and would have fought to the death if the emperor of Japan had not called out, 'Stop, Fire and Water, stop!' Children, our Perfect Emperor played with the crickets all day long. He sent ships to fetch more crickets and men to train them. He built a stable for his crickets and he took the two dragons that guarded the timestick tree and decreed that henceforth they would guard his crickets."

"What a dummy," said Molly. She glanced over her shoulder to make certain the subway entrance had not disappeared. How far away it looked!

The tortoise shut his eyes and opened them again.

"One terrible night the Firebrat crept into our temple. He picked all the timesticks and stowed them in his swordship. By the next morning there was not a trace of the Firebrat, or the Mountain of One Hundred Tempers, or our timesticks."

"What's a swordship?" asked Sean.

"May you never see one," replied the tortoise. "May you never feel its fires nor behold its blades. May your life be as clear as a crystal pillow."

"A what?" asked Molly.

"Don't hurry me," said the tortoise, "or I'll mix everything up. The First Magician on our island had a pillow that sent him truthful dreams. And his dream showed him, across two oceans and under a vast city, the Firebrat in his magic forge, and he was wearing our timesticks in his crown. Children, the swords he tempers by the light of the timesticks will never wear out as long as the Firebrat lives."

Ahead of them Molly spied a small building. Perhaps that's a guardhouse, she thought. She hoped the palace was nearby and that a swift-footed servant would serve them a cool drink of lemonade. It is easier to consider your fate when you are not hot and thirsty and tired.

"Our magician's magic was not strong enough to fly us over the water. So he drew his dream, and he ordered the dream to be frosted on a thousand cookies," rasped the tortoise. "When everyone in our kingdom had eaten one, he changed us into creatures of the sea. To each of us he fastened a neverhunger apple and the seed of a crystal in its tiny house. Our magician took the shape of a golden carp. Halfway over the water he was caught in a net the Firebrat made from a strong spell. We do not know what became of him. And this is terrible, for only our magician knew the spell that could turn us back into ourselves. But the timesticks are wearing out, children. That is why we have so looked forward to your coming. And when you have conquered the Firebrat—"

"Wait!" cried Sean. "We didn't say we would conquer anyone."

"But why else would you have come?" asked the tortoise. "Children, behold the palace!"

Both Molly and Sean stared. There was no palace, only an abandoned kiosk on which the words *candy gum cigars cough drops* showed faintly on the peeling posters and the faded blue paint.

"I don't see any palace," said Molly, very much disappointed.

"Try to imagine it," pleaded the tortoise. "Who knows? Maybe our wishing will bring a little of it back. Places abandoned for a long time take on their own life."

He sounded so mournful that Molly felt sorry for him. She could almost see the silver staircases winding among terraced gardens, the sapphire dragonflies and emerald birds darting to and fro, and the men and women in shimmering robes strolling under the crystal trees.

"Behold the Perfect Emperor!" rasped the tortoise.

A door in the kiosk opened and out swam a fish, scaled in diamonds and wearing a cloak of roses. His face was covered by a torn Dracula mask. Why, it looks like the

mask Eugene took for a friend, thought Molly. She could not imagine how it had arrived here.

When the fish caught sight of Molly and Sean, he balanced on the tip of his tail—he was nearly as tall as a six-year-old child—and turned so that his left eye sparkled at them. With his frilled fins he lifted to his eye a toy spyglass.

"Do tell the Perfect Emperor how handsome he looks in his new face," whispered the tortoise. "He's wearing it so he'll look human."

"But he doesn't look human at all!" exclaimed Molly.

"It was the only face available," said the tortoise. "If you would bow to the Perfect Emperor, he would be so pleased."

Molly bowed, but Sean was so astonished he could only gape at the Perfect Emperor, who lowered his spyglass and shrilled, "I have heard it said that somewhere in the world lives a spell so powerful it can turn timesticks into stars and restore the lost shape of things. If we had such a spell, we would no longer need the timesticks. You wouldn't happen to have that spell with you, would you?"

"Look here," said Molly. "We're not magicians. We were just following the map. We don't want to conquer the Firebrat."

"But you want to go home again, don't you?" said the Perfect Emperor.

"I already told them," said the tortoise gently. "The only way back is through the Firebrat's kingdom."

"Life line, stars, map, destiny—call it what you like," said the Perfect Emperor. "My boat will carry you to the Firebrat. It's waiting for you. You'll have a lovely trip. I'd go myself if I weren't so busy with affairs of state."

As he spoke, the woods around them glittered with the shapes of fish hiding among the branches, listening and watching.

"Perfect Emperor," grumbled the tortoise, "tell them the truth. The road to the Firebrat's forge is full of his creatures, and they are so frightful that even he hates to travel there alone. And *he* shouldn't be afraid of anything, for he put them there himself, and he has the deathdrum to warn him of danger, and on his shoulder he carries the Red Crow that can burn anything, and he commands Killkeep, the sword that—"

"I don't think I want to go," said Molly. "Couldn't you send someone else?"

The Perfect Emperor was used to getting his own way and paid no attention.

"I shall send you in my own boat, and I shall give you my own crew, the best mates that ever sailed the River of Two Kingdoms."

He handed the spyglass to Sean, who put it to his eye. Off in the distance a river sparkled among the trees. On the river bobbed a white boat with sails as thin as tissue.

"Let me see," said Molly, and she raised the spyglass. "Why, there's a whole crowd of people in the boat, and they're waving at us!"

"Perfect Emperor, tell them the truth," said the tortoise. "Your boat is made of paper and so is the crew. Their paper hands are fluttering in the breeze. Our timesticks burn out, our people disappear, and we paint them the way we remember them. We made the memory boat to comfort us, not to carry us."

"But it's the only boat we have!" exclaimed the Perfect Emperor.

"It has never carried the living," the tortoise reminded him. "Some helpful guide should go with them."

"Right," said the Perfect Emperor. "Who in my kingdom will go with the young magicians to conquer the Firebrat?"

His voice rang from branch to branch, like a bird brushing this tree, that tree. Silver glittered in the dark spaces between the trees.

Not a fish came forward. Molly cast a longing glance at the road of pavement which led back to the stairs.

"If there's no other exit," said Molly, "we'll have to go."

"Maybe there *is* another exit," whispered Sean. "One that doesn't lead through the Firebrat's kingdom. And maybe we'll find it."

"Though I am old and a little slow, children, I am still useful," said the tortoise. "Pull a bit of moss from my shell. Carefully."

Sean pulled a large patch of moss from the shell, and revealed four tiny doors. For a moment he was sure he had never seen anything so mysterious and which promised so many secrets.

"How wonderful!" exclaimed Molly, who loved little boxes with compartments.

"Open a door," said the tortoise modestly. "Any door."

Sean opened one, and a Band-Aid dropped out of a small compartment. Molly opened another, and out rolled an apple.

"Band-Aids, neverhunger apples, safety pins—I know what you need before you do," said the tortoise. "Take me with you. I'll carry you when you are tired."

"And I shall see you off with the proper songs and ceremonies," said the Perfect Emperor.

And so it happened that Molly and Sean climbed into the memory boat, which did not look strong enough to hold a shadow, and the paper crew fluttered, and the tortoise paddled starboard, and the Perfect Emperor plucked roses from his cloak and threw them into the water as the boat glided under the trees that lined both sides of the riverbank like watchers at a procession. Long after the emperor was lost from sight, they heard him singing, as if the song itself could protect them:

> *"Roses, roses, I send you home.*
> *Today you blossom, tomorrow you are gone."*

All around them light brightened the leaves of the trees on the banks of the river, and the currents of water cut diamond capers, and the fluttering banners might have been sails of the finest silk. No birds sang. The hum of a locust faded.

"This doesn't feel like a dangerous place," said Molly.

"It's nothing compared to rock climbing with my dad," said Sean. "This place is peaceful."

Good spot for a nap, thought Molly. She felt sleepy. Sean too was yawning. A silvery mist was turning the trees into luminous ghosts. Though the forest was thick, the trunks and branches seemed almost transparent here—yes, she could look right through the trees that grew along the riverbank to the trees behind them.

"I wonder if we might stop and rest a little?" murmured the tortoise. "I did not think the water would weary me so much."

Molly peered down at him. Why, she could see the weedy bottom of the river right through his body! Bewildered, she turned to Sean, who was dozing with his head on his arm. Through his body shone the prow itself.

"Sean, you're fading away!"

Sean sat up and rubbed his eyes and found that his hands were growing clear as glass. He could see through them to Molly's face.

"You're fading too!" he exclaimed. "You're turning into a . . . window."

Behind her face the trees were paling into one another and vanishing. Sean tried to shout, but his voice was as thin as a grasshopper's.

"Tortoise, help us. Carry us out of here."

But the tortoise had grown too light to carry anybody. A faint etching of himself floated on the surface of the river.

"If you come ashore," sang a strong, friendly voice, "you'll come back to yourselves again."

"Where are you?" whispered Sean.

"I'm right at the end of this line," purred the voice. "Don't you see the thread I've thrown over the water?"

All three of them saw it now: a bright thread sparkling on the waves near the boat.

"Touch nothing till we know who's at the other end," cautioned the tortoise, but Molly had already grabbed the line.

The moment she did so, their boat was yanked toward

the shore, and the same voice sang—and it sounded less friendly:

"Thread, thread, haul 'em in!"

A spider squatting among the reeds was reeling them in. She was half as tall as Sean, and she wore a black velvet suit and a chain of silver across her middle, and from the chain swung a red hourglass, which brightened as she wound her thread on its silver reel and grinned.

"Thread, thread, tie 'em up!"

The thread leaped from Molly's hand and tied her feet, and spun around and bound Sean, and dipped into the water and trussed the tortoise.

Then it dragged the three prisoners to the spider and laid them at all her feet.

"It's been ages since anyone has passed," said the spider. "I hope you're not poisonous. I'm famished."

"We'd make rather a thin meal," said the tortoise. "Just look at us."

"I'm looking," said the spider. "You look delicious. You've left the Waters of Waning behind you."

"The Waters of Waning?" said Sean.

"You waned, did you not?" asked the spider. "And now that you've left the Waters of Waning, you're plumping out again. Of course, your boat is gone."

"Oh, our boat!" cried Molly.

The boat had vanished without a trace.

"It's waned clean away," said the spider. "Get moving."

"If we'd looked before we leaped," sighed the tortoise, "we might have saved the boat. But it's too late now."

They left the river behind and hobbled into the forest, first Molly, and next Sean, and finally the tortoise, huffing and puffing, for he could hardly keep up the pace that the spider set as she scampered ahead of them. From time to time she gave a little tug on the thread, which was sticky as well as strong, as if the spider had smeared it with juice taken from some evil-smelling flower. She stopped at a hole that led straight under the roots of a tree.

"Home sweet home," cackled the spider. "After you."

"We can't even fit through the door," said Sean.

"Get down on your knees and try," snapped the spider.

On hands and knees Molly and Sean entered the dark passage, in which nothing could be heard but the tortoise's words of comfort: "Don't be afraid, children. When the dark tries to scare you, scare it back. And remember: the dark never stays. I shall sing something to give us courage. I shall sing our national anthem:

"This is daylight's finest hour—"

"Quiet down there!" roared the spider just as the tunnel made a sharp turn and they tumbled into her lair.

A faint yellow light from the smoke hole threw their shadows across the floor, which was littered with wings, eyes, and broken bodies of insects chewed beyond recognition. Fine gray rags covered everything, like tattered shrouds, which might have trapped them or wrapped them once. A giant toadstool hung from the low ceiling.

It was worse than any room Molly had ever seen, including her own.

"Gross," said Sean. "Really gross."

"You can't judge character by a messy room," said the spider, and she slid the hourglass from the silver chain around her middle and turned it to let the sand run through. Then she hung it on a root that dangled beside the toadstool.

By a circle of stones under the smoke hole stood a portable sewing machine, snarled over with threads. The spider kicked the machine aside as she brisked about the room.

"Ah, there's my tripod and my pot," she muttered, "but I can't find my sticks, I can't find my poker. It's too crowded. I need more room, more room."

"If you picked up your dirty clothes, you'd have a lot more room," said Molly. And she thought at the same moment, Am I saying that? I sound like my mother.

"These are not dirty clothes," said the spider. She picked up a ball of tangled threads and ignited it with the light from her hourglass. Over the fire she set her pot.

"These are webs. Old webs. Scraps. Too nice to throw away. I traded all my best webs for this sewing machine."

"They're hideous," said Molly. "They look like Grandma's doilies. But she does hers in colors."

The spider sighed deeply.

"I've never been able to achieve color," she said. "But with this new machine, I'm going to try. It does all the traditional patterns: Flower Garden, Log Cabin, Smashed Wasp, Broken Wing. Believe me, miss, a lot of work goes into these webs."

"I understand," said the tortoise. "A lot of work goes into my shell, too. How fortunate that you didn't eat us on sight. You have at your service two powerful magicians from the Upper World."

"Where are they?" asked the spider.

"You are in the presence of the Most Noble Magician Molly and the Most Serviceable Sorcerer Sean. Ask the Noble Molly to consult her book of spells."

The spider made a little bow.

"O Most Noble Magician Molly, will you consult your book of spells?"

"I don't have a book of spells," said Molly. "I mean, I don't have it with me."

"With salt and pepper you'd be delicious," muttered the spider. "I believe magicians are considered a delicacy."

"You must have it," said the tortoise. "I saw it myself in your pocket."

"He means Eugene's book," whispered Sean. *"How to Fix Everything!* Get it out quick, Moll."

"Or raw," said the spider in a dreamy tone. "Or baked in a sauce of pickled bee stings."

Molly felt in her pocket and whisked out *How to Fix Everything!*

"You see," crowed the tortoise, "she does have a book. Molly, find the spell for mending webs."

"There's a section on invisible reweaving," faltered Molly. But what good would it do here? she thought.

"Same thing," said the tortoise. "Read on."

Molly opened the book. There it was. The art of invisible reweaving. But the words on the page had nothing to do with mending rips in one's clothes, and when Molly read them she was not quite sure what would happen next.

"Ah tsaekfa!" read Molly.

Instantly all the broken threads in the spider's lair sat up and took notice.

"Ananse, ananse, ananse!" Molly continued.

The threads shivered and shimmered. On a loom of air they bowed to their partners, whirled over rips and under tears, darted back and forth, twang, twang! They danced, they fluttered, they flew.

All at once they gathered together and hung themselves on the walls in an exquisite embroidery of hollyhocks and starflowers, smashed wasps bathed in moonlight, broken wings shimmering in the rain.

Molly dropped the book in astonishment.

"You're wonderful," the tortoise told her. "Simply wonderful."

The spider made a little purring sound.

"My mother always said I had talent. I can't thank you enough for all you've done. If there's anything I can do for you—"

"You can let us go," said Sean.

"Every night I tell myself a bedtime story," said the spider softly, "about a hungry spider who captures three travelers and eats them. It's my favorite story. I go to bed hungry every night."

"I know a story about a wise, kind spider who catches three travelers and lets them go," said Molly. "That's my favorite story."

"Just my luck," sighed the spider. "I finally catch a really good meal. I find my pot and my embers, and suddenly we're friends."

"If you don't let us go," said Sean, "Molly will say a spell that will tie you up for good. Right, Molly?"

And he snatched the book.

"Children, children," said the tortoise, "open the door over my left leg and give our friend a neverhunger apple and some grapes."

Molly opened the door and reached into the little compartment and brought out an apple, ripened to perfection.

"I don't see any grapes," she said.

"Pity," said the tortoise. "I was sure I'd packed some."

And so it happened that the spider untied her prisoners, and Molly and Sean and the tortoise and the spider sat down to share the neverhunger apple, which had grown near the timestick tree and never lost its sweetness. A single bite from that apple tasted of the food that each loved best and took away the very memory of hunger and put them all in a better humor.

"We would be most grateful," said the tortoise, "if you could tell us where we are."

The spider set the apple—which had grown whole again—on the sewing machine and wiped her mouth with the back of one leg.

"Well, you're lost, or you wouldn't be here. You're in the Firebrat's forest."

"Do you know where we can find him?" asked Molly.

"Why do you want to find him?"

"He stole a great treasure from my people," said the tortoise, "and we want to bring it back."

"Treasure, treasure," muttered the spider, shutting her eyes. "Well, you'll have to take the train into the Dark's country. What lies beyond the Dark I don't know. Nobody has ever come back to tell about it."

"A train in the forest!" exclaimed Sean. "How often does it run?"

"Oh, it runs all the time," answered the spider, "if it is a train. I've never seen it, but I've heard it plenty of times. And believe me, I run for cover."

"Wh—what does it sound like?" asked Molly.

"It roars," replied the spider. She opened her eyes wide.

"Perhaps it's a lion," suggested the tortoise.

"Or a train of lions," added Sean. "Does it leave tracks?"

"It doesn't need to. There are tracks all over the forest. Train tracks from the old days before the Firebrat. He doesn't keep the place up anymore. His magic is only plated on, and the plate is wearing thin in spots."

"If it runs on tracks, then it's certainly a train," said Molly.

"I didn't say it ran on tracks," the spider corrected her. "It runs on wheels, and the wheels leave big ruts in the ground."

Silence.

"Where can we catch this train—if it is a train?" asked the tortoise.

"I can show you the clearing," said the spider, "where it comes to drink."

"To drink!" exclaimed Molly and Sean with one voice.

"And when you hear it coming, run after it and jump aboard."

"Won't the conductor stop?" asked Sean.

"What conductor?" said the spider. "This train is alive. And if it's in a good humor, it will take you at least as far as the Dark's country."

"And if it's in a bad humor?" whispered Molly.

"Watch out," said the spider. "It will chase you all over the forest."

And she scampered out of the cave.

The three travelers followed her, and they walked for some distance without speaking, afraid of what their voices might waken.

We could leave the spider, thought Molly, and look for another way out. But what if there were none? They could lose themselves here forever.

The spider broke the silence.

"Do you see that pool ahead of us? That's where the train comes to drink."

In the distance lazed a murky pond on which lay a film of rainbows from an oil slick.

"Farewell," said the tortoise, "and thanks for all your help."

"Good-bye," said the spider.

And she handed Molly a small gray parcel.

"What's this you're giving us?" asked Molly.

"A powerful web," replied the spider, "to remember me by."

"Oh, we'll remember you all right," said Sean.

"In your hour of need, this web will help you. It's a very sensible web. If you need a bridge, it's a bridge. If you need a road, it's a road. And it folds up real small."

"Thank you," said Molly, taking the parcel. She wanted to shake hands, but it seemed too complicated.

"I never travel without a web," added the spider. "You never know when one might come in handy."

Not until the spider had disappeared into the shadows did they set off toward the pond. Though the air was still, they heard the trickling of water. As they tramped along, the trees that had looked so luminous from the boat threw a net of shadows over them. The ground was bare; neither grass nor flowers grew there, only an occasional toadstool, dead white.

"What I miss most are the birds," said the tortoise. "The birds on our island sang the most exquisite songs. There was no end of music."

In the silence, something rumbled far off, as though a storm were brewing. Yet it did not sound exactly like thunder. Molly thought of the subway platform and the trains rushing through the darkness, beaming their lights on the walls. And presently they felt the earth begin to shake under their feet.

"Children, stand fast," said the tortoise. "I will protect you."

The rumble rose to an insistent pounding, a humming and hissing, a clicking and clatter that burst into a siren, as two beams of light shot toward them and something burst into the clearing.

It was an old fire engine that must have been pulled by horses once, for traces of the shafts bumped along the ground, and smoke and sparks streamed from the rusty boiler stack, while the bell clanged and the whistle shrieked and the tattered hose dragged after it like a tail.

The fire engine screeched up to the pond, dipped in its hose, and slurped.

"Why, it's nothing but an old wreck," said Sean. "We can't go anywhere in that."

The fire engine lifted its hose like an elephant contemplating mischief. Its headlights winked this way and that, and a deep, scratchy voice from the depths of the engine roared, "Who said that?"

"I meant to say, we can't go anywhere till you've finished drinking," quavered Sean.

The fire engine impaled them on a beam of light. Then it sent a stream of dirty water shooting over them and roared with laughter.

"You should give up water," said the tortoise. "It's bad for your digestion. Just look at you, rusting to pieces, a fine fellow like yourself."

"At the count of three," said the fire engine, "I run you over."

"Climb aboard, children. Quickly!"

"One—"

Sean scrambled aboard and Molly followed. Glancing down, she saw the tortoise pawing helplessly at the front wheel.

"Two—"

"Sean, we have to help the tortoise!"

She jumped down and tried to lift him.

"Push me onto the shafts below the boiler," said the tortoise.

No sooner had they eased him into the wooden shafts than the fire engine bawled "Three!" and Molly clambered back up into the driver's seat and pulled Sean after her.

"We'd like to go—" she shouted over the shriek of the whistle, but the fire engine drowned her out.

"Nobody tells me where to go!"

Into the darkness it crashed, throwing off sparks, knocking down bushes and small trees, singeing branches, and spewing forth smoke in such clouds that Sean was gasping for breath and Molly thought she would choke.

He's trying to bump us off, thought Molly, just like an ornery horse.

She peered down at the tortoise. He had retreated into his shell.

At last the fire engine slowed down.

"Where are we?" asked Sean.

"Back where we started," said Molly. "The fire engine has been running in circles."

The fire engine growled.

"The Firebrat made me," it rumbled. "He made me to start fires, not to put them out. He made me out of knives and lost tempers. I look good, but I'm mean inside. Don't trust me. Oh, don't trust me."

"Where does the Firebrat live?" asked Sean.

"Haven't seen him for years," rasped the fire engine. "When I was new, he used to drive me about the woods for fun. But he left me to rust, and afterward he put me out to fend for myself. He likes things that shine. If

only I knew how to shine! If only I could shake off this rust—"

"If you take us to the Firebrat, we'll take off your rust," said Sean.

"You!" snorted the fire engine. "You, without even a siren or wheels."

"How fortunate for you that you found us," said the tortoise, drawing out of his shell. "You have at your service two powerful magicians from the Upper World."

Sean was thumbing through *How to Fix Everything!* "Rust, rust," he muttered to himself. "Mildew, stains— I found it! How to get rid of rust!"

The fire engine quivered.

"Can you really do that?" it whispered. "Can you really make me as good as new?"

"It's right here in the book," said Sean. " 'How to Banish Rust.' "

"Say the spell," urged Molly.

Sean read:

> *"Shine come in and Sorrow go.*
> *In this spell I put my trust.*
> *Farewell, dents and dirt and rust.*
> *Meshach, Master of the Fire,*
> *Shadrach, Shepherd of the Dust,*
> *Rot and Ruin, climb no higher.*
> *Shine come in and Sorrow go,*
> *Shadrach and Abednego."*

A curious scratching was heard, as if invisible hands were scrubbing the fire engine, which stood perfectly still, like a cat being stroked. Flakes of rust blew this way and that.

At last the fire engine said in low tones, "Do you see any shine?"

"I see some there, on your back fender," said Molly.

"And here's a little coming through on your boiler," said Sean. "I can see my face in it."

Scrabble, scrabble, scritch, scratch. Around the fire engine, rust powdered the ground.

"Look in the pond," said the tortoise.

The fire engine drew itself up alongside the pond and gave a little grunt of pleasure.

"Wait till the Firebrat sees me," it growled. "Just wait."

"Can you take us to the Firebrat?" asked Molly.

"I can take you as far as the swamp," replied the fire engine. "I won't go any farther. I'm scared of the Dark."

"But you've got your lights," said Sean.

"You don't know the Dark," answered the fire engine. "My lights can't touch him. Ordinary dark is like shutting your eyes. It's like playing hide-and-seek with the world, and the world doesn't go away. But the Dark I'm speaking of is a thief, a monster, a—who knows what? No one has seen him. But if you're unlucky enough to meet him—"

The fire engine's headlights glanced around nervously.

"What happens?" asked Molly.

"He'll suck the life out of you," whispered the fire engine. "His breath is as cold as a thousand winters piled one on top of another. And he's fussy, the Dark is. All his trees are wired. If you break off so much as a single twig, he knows. He can hear the breath of spiders. He can hear the turning of a single page. And he's there in an instant."

Sean shivered and dropped the book. All around them, the twilight was deepening.

"Dim your lights," said Sean, "so the Dark can't see us."

"Of course he can't see us," said the fire engine. "He's as blind as a mole. But he can hear us. Lord, can he hear! You have to cross the swamp without the Dark hearing you if you want to reach the other side."

"How will we know when we've reached it?" asked Molly.

"Follow the tracks to the stairs that lead to the Earthen Lake," replied the fire engine. "Now get down. This is as far as I go."

The travelers helped each other down.

"We'll be very quiet," said the tortoise.

"Good," said the fire engine. "Let me give you a rousing send-off."

The fire engine rang its bells, gunned its motor, blew its sirens, belched black smoke, and sang at the top of its voice. "Hey, hey! Folks in the woods! Folks going to find the Firebrat!"

"Shush!" cried Molly. "Are you crazy?"

"Dark, Dark, come this way! Folks in the woods, night and day," roared the fire engine.

"You promised you'd help us," Sean blazed out.

"Did not," snickered the fire engine.

"That's not fair," said Molly. "We helped you."

The fire engine was laughing wildly.

"Didn't I tell you I was made from knives? Didn't I tell you not to trust me?"

They heard him shrieking and whooping after them, "Dark, Dark, there's folks in the woods!" as they fled terrified into the swamp.

The ghastly light of the fox-fire burning cold on the black water, the vines dangling from trees taller than gallows, the air still and hot and smelling of decay, a branch rotting here, there, falling, sinking, as the water closed over it: the swamp. Molly stepped on a log, which shifted, opened its jaws, and snapped at her.

"Walk on the weedy hummocks, children!" cried the tortoise. "You have no shell to protect you."

Sean paused, searching for the best path, and the deadly nightshade shook its purple flowers and tangled itself around his feet. The sword grass was shredding his sneakers, and half a dozen eyes glowed among the thin blades, watching him.

Around them the trees gave off a pale green glow, and a deadly beauty infected the ground and speckled it with lights. Lights? They were toadstools: avenging angels, dead man's fingers, death cap. How harmless they'd looked on Grandma's TV and how hostile they felt to Molly now.

"Tracks!" shouted Sean. "I stepped on tracks!"

"Hush!" hissed Molly. "Where?"

"Here."

At his feet a tiny arc of steel gleamed for an instant where he had kicked the grass aside. As they bent for a closer look, the blades shifted and closed over it.

"Children," said the tortoise, "you will find candles in the compartment over my right leg. The Dark can't see them."

Molly opened the little door and took out two candles.

"But there are no matches," she said.

"For these candles, none are needed," the tortoise assured her. "A breath lights them, a breath snuffs them out."

Molly handed one to Sean, then took a deep breath and blew over the wicks. A warm flame sprang to life on each of them.

"I see another bit of track," said Sean. "Give me a knife and I'll slash our way out of here."

"Don't cut anything, don't break anything, for heaven's sake!" cried the tortoise. "We're almost free. Isn't that the stairway to the Earthen Lake?"

Half a dozen yards ahead of them, a narrow flight of stone steps led into the ground. The branches were now so thick that Molly could make no progress. For every branch she pushed aside, two clawed their way into the space, till at last a branch curved like a hook reached out and clutched her by the hair. The more Molly tried to work it loose, the tighter it held her, and in a fury of impatience, she jerked the strands free.

A twig snapped.

A shiver ran through the swamp, and the tree uttered a shrill howl. Molly shrieked and dropped her candle, which immediately went out.

"Don't be afraid," said the tortoise. "Climb aboard. Light your candle again, my dear. I shall find a way around these branches."

They huddled on the high curve of his shell, tucking their legs under them, Molly in front, holding her candle high, Sean behind her, watching over his shoulder for—he hardly knew what. As they neared the stairs, a friendly light seemed to rise before them. They could breathe easier now. They were nearly out of the swamp.

Suddenly the candles shyed out. Sean's breath whitened to a crackle of frost. Molly felt her bones turn to ice and gave a cry of pain.

"Children," gasped the tortoise, "run for the stairs. I will fend off the Dark."

"We can't leave you," said Sean.

"I have my shell. Wait for me. When the Dark has passed, I'll find you."

Sean and Molly dropped their candles and fled to the

stairs. Kneeling on the top step, they saw the tortoise's candle twinkle to life like a friendly star.

The next instant a huge black wing stretched over the tortoise, brushed the flame out, and swept toward them.

"Get down!" hissed Sean.

With a roar like a tidal wave, the Dark beat his wings and loosened the winds of a thousand winters, which tore through the forest and stripped the trees bare and lashed at every living thing it could find on the surface of the earth.

Just below the surface, on the stairway to the Earthen Lake, crouched Molly and Sean.

And then the Dark groaned and folded his wings and drew himself back like a tide, flowing back among the trees, into the swamp, and the warm air returned, and the trees began to put out new leaves.

By tree light and grass light, the tortoise's shell resembled a strange planet.

"It's all right, dear friend," called Sean. "The Dark is gone."

No friendly head showed itself. Molly ran out with Sean at her heels, and together they peered into the tortoise's shell.

Empty. Sucked dry, as simple and mysterious as a skull.

Molly threw herself down on the ground and burst into tears. Never had the universe felt so hostile, and never had she felt so alone.

"How can we go on without the tortoise?" she wailed. "He was so good to us. He took care of us."

But through her tears she saw brambles creeping over the empty shell, tying it to the earth, and she felt vines looping themselves around her feet.

"Get up, Molly, fast! Let's take the shell and get out of here. And get the candles."

Together they ripped at the stems and tendrils. When they'd freed the shell and Molly could move her feet, they searched for the candles.

"I can only find one of them," said Molly. "That's better than nothing."

She blew on the wick and Sean cupped the flame with his hands.

Suddenly the air at their backs turned sharply cold. There on the path was the Dark, his huge wings folded quietly at his sides. He seemed to be sleeping. They could hear him snoring softly.

The Dark drew a deep breath, and the candle he held flared. Molly was sure it was the tortoise's candle.

"Only the tortoise," she said, "would give a night light to the Dark."

The stairs led straight down to the shores of an amber lake in a cave so vast they could almost believe they'd returned to the upper world. The sapphires studding the dome glittered like stars on a summer night, and the scarlet glow over the cliffs on the opposite shore might have been the setting sun.

"The Firebrat—I'm sure that's where the Firebrat lives," said Molly.

As if the cliffs heard her, they began to glow, and a road of red light shimmered on the surface of the lake. It led from where they stood to the other side. Directly across from them appeared a door labeled FIRE EXIT, over which flashed a sign: SOUTH FERRY.

"Sean—we're saved! There *is* another way home!"

A smell of onion rolls wafted across the water.

"Maybe my mom is buying rolls on the way home from work," said Sean.

Music from a radio on the far side of the door startled them both.

> *"I'd like to be under the sea*
> *in an octopus's garden in the shade.*
> *He'd let us in, knows where we've been,*
> *in his octopus's garden in the shade."*

"Oh, Sean, let's take that road home," pleaded Molly. "It's our only chance. We have no boat. We can't go back the way we came. That silly little emperor isn't worth getting killed over. What difference does it make, now that the tortoise is gone?"

They glanced down at the shell. A small door was opening near the center. Sean reached inside and brought out a handkerchief. It rustled and creaked and stretched and swelled into a sail.

"I think the tortoise wants us to go on," said Sean quietly. "Didn't he ask us to save his people? Didn't he ask us to bring back the timesticks?"

Molly was silent. The road, the door, the sign faded, until nothing remained but the lake.

"He wants us to use his shell for a boat," added Sean.

"I don't know anything about sailing," said Molly impatiently.

"I do. My dad showed me. Only problem is, there's no wind."

The door to a second compartment opened, and Molly took out a spyglass and a leathern bag. From the string dangled a tag: ONE FAIR WIND.

Together they pushed the shell into the water and seated themselves on the flat underside. Sean opened the bag. With a glad whoosh, the wind tumbled out, and the shell nearly capsized. Right to the middle of the lake they flew.

Now the wind was content to puff docilely behind them. Molly lifted the spyglass to her eye and turned it this way and that.

"What do you see?" Sean asked.

"I see a big red bird flying toward the cliff with a book in its beak."

"Let me look," said Sean, and Molly handed him the spyglass.

"What do you see?" she asked.

"I see a lovely frog on the shore at the very end of the lake."

"Let me see," said Molly.

In the round eye of the spyglass shimmered no common frog but a pulsing emerald.

"Molly," said Sean, "something funny is happening to the lake."

As if someone had pulled a plug, the water level was falling and the steep sides of the basin began to wall them in. The wrecked spars and masts of old ships broke through the water on all sides.

"And—oh, Sean, something is happening to the frog!"

The frog was swelling to ten, fifteen, twenty times its size and gulping down the lake in enormous swallows, and each swallow stretched the frog a little more till through its emerald skin they could see the waves sloshing to and fro.

Now the frog was as big as a house, and now as big as a castle, and the tortoise's shell rested on a mud flat at the bottom of the lake, among skiffs, rowboats, train tracks, even a small graveyard.

"Get the magic book!" screamed Molly.

Before Sean could answer, a gray thread floated out of Molly's pocket. One end fastened itself to the tortoise's shell while the other soared over the empty lake bed and touched down on the opposite shore.

"The spider's web!" exclaimed Molly.

The thread was weaving itself into a silken bridge. No sooner had Molly and Sean climbed aboard the web and pulled the tortoise's shell after them than the web started to rise. Rolling the shell before them, they bounced over the bridge toward the glowing cliffs of the Firebrat's kingdom just as the frog opened its mouth and the whole lake roared after them and slammed them against the shore.

Molly sat up. Though she was drenched from head to toe, she found herself still clutching the spyglass, or what was left of it; the bottom half was sheared away. Close beside her, Sean lay sprawled over the tortoise's shell.

Under the sapphire dome, which brushed a soft brilliance over everything, the lake was perfectly still and showed no further interest in the two travelers it had tossed under the red cliffs, plain and polished as an apple.

"I feel like one big toothache," said Sean. "Everything hurts."

"What's that in your hand?" asked Molly.

"The spider's web. And it isn't even torn." He stuffed it into his pocket.

Clang, clang, clang! Both of them heard it: the ring of a hammer on steel.

The next moment a boisterous voice roared:

"Today we starve, tomorrow we feast,
Walk-in doctor, man or beast,
Old for new and new for old,
Iron, copper, silver, gold."

Molly and Sean looked at each other in alarm.

"Is that the Firebrat?" whispered Molly.

"I don't know," said Sean. "It's coming from inside the cliff."

Suddenly an opening appeared at the base of the cliffs, and a long streak of light spilled over the rocks like a road paved in honey.

Clang, clang, clang!

"Let's find out who it is," said Sean.

"What if it's the Firebrat?"

"What if it's not?"

At the crack in the cliff, they stopped. Holding her breath, Molly peeked in. What she saw so astonished her that she forgot her fear and exclaimed, "Sean, look!"

A pair of golden hands was working away at an anvil, hammering something that glinted and gleamed by the light of a furnace that blazed in the middle of the room. And what a furnace! The chimney with its fiery chamber was cut from the cliff itself and rose so high that neither Molly nor Sean could see the top. On the walls hung tongs and mallets and hammers—big hammers and bigger hammers, little hammers and tiny hammers. Around the furnace, as if warming themselves, huddled other anvils, great and small, like horses waiting to be shod.

The left hand laid the hammer aside, the right hand held up the work: a golden bird.

"Molly," whispered Sean, "on the left hand—Eugene's ring!"

Sure enough, on the middle finger of the left hand the blue eye under its silver lid glanced this way and that and finally rested its gaze on Molly and Sean, while the hand carried the golden bird to the fire and tossed it in.

"Oh, don't!" cried Molly.

Did the bird care? No, indeed. It flew singing out of the fire and darted about the room like a star and perched at last on an old tin lantern that swung out from the wall on a fat chain.

"It's the bird from the music box in Grandma's shop," said Sean joyfully. "Is Eugene here? Eugene?" he called. "It's us! Can you get us out of here?"

The golden hands beckoned them forward, and a hollow voice announced, "Fair trade. A spyglass for armor—"

Molly hesitated, then laid the broken spyglass on the anvil.

"—armor, proof against the Firebrat."

"Give me armor that will make me as brave as a samurai," begged Sean.

"Does the dung beetle wear gold?" demanded the voice. "Does the snail wear silver? Bring the armor that was given to you. Bring me the shell of the tortoise."

Molly ran to fetch it. There it lay on the rocks, its moss hanging down on all sides in ragged strips. She rolled it right up to the anvil, where the golden hands lifted the shell and tapped it—click, click, click—and the voice sang like water stirring at the bottom of a well:

> *"Save their feet from the deathdrum,*
> *Save their arms for the work to be done,*
> *Save their eyes from the Red Crow,*
> *Save their hearts from Killkeep the Sword."*

The shell snipped and snapped and turned and twisted. And now the armor was finished, and the greaves and gauntlets and helmets assembled themselves, and two complete suits of armor turned to face Molly and Sean, like secret shells of themselves.

"Now put on your armor," commanded the voice.

Sean had no sooner buckled on his armor than it disappeared. Molly put on hers and it melted away under her fingers.

"This armor won't work," said Sean. "It doesn't stay."

The voice chuckled.

"Yes, it does. But you can't feel or see it. Do you want to go clattering around the world in a tortoise shell?"

"What good is armor if the Firebrat can't see it?" asked Molly.

"You don't wear armor to please your enemy," said the voice. "You wear it to protect yourself. Be as slow and brave as the tortoise. Slow to anger. Slow to run away. Now put your hands in your pockets. What do you find?"

"Safety pins," said Sean.

"A neverhunger apple," said Molly.

"Put them back and let them go. They'll come back when they're called."

The fire in the furnace was dying. The anvils, the hammers, indeed the hands themselves were fading into the darkness.

"Go now," said the voice. The right hand gave Molly a gentle push, and the left hand tugged Sean outside. When they turned back to say good-bye, Molly and Sean saw no forge, no fire, no golden hands—nothing but the high, bare cliffs.

"I'll bet Eugene is behind this," said Sean.

"Then why didn't he get us out of here? There's no way up that cliff. We should have taken the road to the fire exit."

Sean ran his hands over the side of the cliff.

"When I went rock climbing with my dad, we went up lots of cliffs just as smooth as this. You can almost always find a niche to put your foot in, if you keep looking. Here's a foothold—a little one—but it's enough."

And he jammed his foot into the tiny niche and hoisted himself up.

Toes wedged into crevices, fingers clutched at fissures. Straight up the cliff they climbed, inching forward, resting, digging in, moving on, like small animals. When they pulled themselves over the last ledge, they stretched out, exhausted.

Below them spread a lake of molten rock, blazing and bubbling—oh, there was no end of fire shooting high into the air like flaming fountains, no end of the boiling and crackling, no end of the rocks raining down and the red-hot lava churning and churning.

And right in the middle of the churning and burning was an island, and in the middle of the island was a fire that danced red and white. And in the middle of the fire?

"It's the Firebrat!" exclaimed Molly.

His whole body glowed. From his antennae flashed lightning, and a fiery wind seemed to rustle through all his legs at once. His bristly tail whipped the fire higher! hotter! He was tempering swords and hanging them on the hooked tails of the flames. And the flames—what were they but fierce, ragged beasts that the Firebrat had pulled from the fire to keep it hot?

On his shoulder rode the Red Crow, and around him spun a giant scimitar, slashing the air as it kept watch over hundreds of sparkling wands that danced in the Firebrat's crown.

"That's Killkeep," whispered Sean. "And those are the timesticks. How can we take back the timesticks unless we catch Killkeep napping?"

"Maybe there's a spell in the book. You had it last, Sean, remember? When we unrusted the fire engine."

"It must have dropped out of my pocket," said Sean in an anguished voice. In that moment he remembered the truth: he'd dropped the book when he was riding the fire engine.

Thump!

Thump!

Thump!

Was it her heart making such a racket? Molly wondered. Or a muffled drumbeat in the earth? The deathdrum? Ashes and smoke darkened the air, and the lake of fire brightened and heaved.

Thump!

Thump!

Thump!

Sean caught her arm, and in the same moment they saw Killkeep streaking toward them, and riding its ruby hilt was the Firebrat himself. On his shoulder the Red Crow had clamped in its beak a book that Molly and Sean recognized at once.

"Killkeep, ring them with fire!"

And the sword threw a rope of flame around Molly and Sean. Hovering over their heads, the Firebrat grinned, and the faceted jewels of his eyes nearly blinded them.

"You thought it would be easy to take my timesticks," he sneered. "You thought you would come with your book of spells and conquer me. Red Crow, break the book!"

And the Red Crow tossed *How to Fix Everything!*

straight into the ring of fire. The pages shrieked and scooted away, no longer pages but tiny firebrats, hundreds of them, bright, fierce, and hungry. They gobbled the flames, and the Firebrat roared with laughter.

"You thought you'd catch my sword asleep? Killkeep never sleeps. You thought you'd sneak past me when my back was turned?"

Killkeep tapped the stones around their feet impatiently.

"Are you tired?" asked the Firebrat. "I keep a chamber especially for my guests. And I haven't had the pleasure of a guest for a long time. Killkeep, show them the dungeon."

The sword struck the ground at their feet, and the ground yawned open. The Red Crow darted at them, Killkeep slashed at them, the Firebrat spat at them, and the earth closed over Molly and Sean.

Thud.

They landed on a dirt floor. As their eyes grew accustomed to the dark, it sparkled here, winked there. Amethysts and rubies gleamed on the walls and the ceiling, which was so low that when Molly stood up, the crystals scraped her head.

"Molly, look—thrones!"

There were twelve of them carved into the circular wall, just like the numbers on a clock. Twelve o'clock was cut from a solid ruby, three o'clock from a block of emeralds, six o'clock from a cluster of diamonds, nine o'clock from a blue sapphire, and the hours in between from blocks of jet. From the quarter hours streamed rays that threw the shapes of flowers onto the floor, like a garden of lights. And on every throne sat a fish wrought of beaten gold, its fins draped on the armrests. Patches of jewels grew on the twelve o'clock and the three o'clock fish, like moss on old tombstones.

"They almost look alive," said Molly. "Feel their scales."

But Sean was standing before the diamond throne as if it had hypnotized him.

"What a beautiful throne," he whispered. "And it's just my size."

"I like the emerald one better," said Molly.

It threw her a glance, a gleam, a promise: choose me and you shall have your heart's desire. All their adventures seemed no more than a dream beside that promise.

"And it's just my size," she added.

She and Sean were about to sit down when a voice hissed, "I beg of you, do not sit!"

Sean sprang back so fast he bumped into Molly, who jumped back at the same moment.

"Who said that?" he shouted.

"If I were in your shoes," continued the voice, "and that would be a fine sight, since I have no feet, I would not sit on those thrones. Unless you want to sit on them forever."

The crystals that were under the diamond throne shivered a little, and a crack opened like a smile, through which glided a black snake. Molly shrieked, and the snake began to tremble.

"If you do that again, I shall flee," hissed the snake. "And if I flee, I can't help you. And who knows when I'll muster enough courage to speak to a human again."

The snake paused, as if it had made an embarrassing confession, and then asked, "Am I in the presence of the Honorable Edna Hester?"

"Edna Hester is my grandmother," said Molly, astonished. "Do you know her?"

"I have not had the pleasure of meeting that noble lady," replied the snake. "But I know her story, for it has slithered down through the generations: the story of how Edna Hester saved the king of the snakes."

Its voice softened, as if it were speaking from a great distance. "Every snake knows the story of how our king glided through the woods to conquer Dog, who killed our queen. Dog seized our king and held him between his teeth and would have killed him if a noble human had not taken him from the jaws of Dog. And ever since, we have celebrated Edna Hester Day, the day our king was delivered from an untimely death."

For several minutes nobody spoke.

"How did you know Molly was here?" asked Sean.

"Because of the rattlesnake ring she wears. We gave that ring long ago to the Honorable Edna Hester. If the

Honorable Edna or any of her descendants rubs the ring, one of the snake folk will appear and grant one wish. Just one. No one has called us until now."

"I didn't know I'd called you," said Molly.

"How fortunate you did," said the snake. "If you or your companion had sat on those thrones, you would never have risen again."

"Like the golden fish," said Sean, shuddering.

"Yes, like the golden fish, who were once crystal people—they tried to rescue the timesticks."

"That's why we've come," said Molly. "To rescue the timesticks."

The snake swayed thoughtfully among the ruby and emerald lights.

"You will have to destroy the Firebrat," it said in the pleasantest voice imaginable.

"And that's impossible," groaned Sean.

"Difficult," agreed the snake, "but not impossible. Take his heart. If you can take the Firebrat's heart, you will have him in your power."

"It would be easier to take the timesticks than his heart," said Molly.

"You are mistaken," said the snake. "The Firebrat's heart is not in his body. It's made of fire opals, and he keeps it in a coffin at the bottom of the Lake of Fire."

"Forget it," said Sean. "I'm not going into the Lake of Fire."

"Why are you afraid?" asked the snake. "You must be

wearing magic armor or you could not have come this far. And once you've found your way into the Lake of Fire, you have only to vanquish the twelve giant salamanders—"

"Giant salamanders!" cried Molly.

"—who guard the coffin that holds the Firebrat's heart. Unfortunately, your armor is not proof against their fire. A friendly handshake and poof! You're a handful of ashes. But if you escape turning to ashes, you have only to take out the Firebrat's heart and pour water on it."

"That's the easy part," said Molly.

"No, that's the hard part," said the snake. "There's not a drop of water in the Firebrat's kingdom. I can lead you to the Lake of Fire, I can help you charm the giant salamanders—for they're relations of mine—but I can't help you bring water to the Lake of Fire. Water doesn't like it here. It simply goes up in steam."

The snake stopped swaying and fixed its bright gaze on Sean.

"Friend of the Honorable Edna, the earth is full of roads, and we snakes know all of them. I know a frog that can help you. I can show you the road to that frog. But the rest is up to you."

"What about me?" asked Molly.

"You will have to find the Firebrat's heart. Only a descendant of the Honorable Edna can pass with favor among my relatives. You wear the ring, and you are one of us by deed and caring. On any other hand the ring is as dead as an old leaf."

Sean frowned.

"What if I can't get any water?"

"Molly will fall under the Firebrat's sword. And not even the king of the snakes can tell when you'll find your way home again."

"Show me the road," said Sean.

The serpent tapped its nose on the space under the sapphire throne, and the crystals parted to reveal a narrow passage.

"This road will take you to the Earthen Lake and to the emerald frog that guards it," said the snake. "You'll travel by gem light till you reach the water."

"Sean, Sean, be careful," called Molly. "If you don't come back, I'm dead."

"Don't worry, Molly," came Sean's voice from deep inside the walls.

And he was gone.

Singing among the reeds at the edge of the lake was the emerald frog.

> *"I am a noble lady.*
> *My pedigree is green.*
> *I have the biggest appetite*
> *the world has ever seen."*

Sean crept forward and grabbed her.

"Let me go! Let me go!" shrieked the frog. "I am poison to the touch!"

Sean hung on.

"A single glance from my glittering eye can kill!" cried the frog.

Sean hung on.

"He who holds me will turn to stone for a thousand years!"

Sean hung on. The frog stopped struggling.

"What do you want?" she pleaded in a small voice.

"I want you to swallow the lake and pour it out over the Firebrat's heart."

The emerald skin paled.

"If I work for you, is the pay good? The Firebrat pays me nothing."

Sean reached into his pocket and took out a safety pin and a subway token, which he set before her. The frog snapped up the pin.

"A very sharp taste," she observed.

Then she gobbled up the token.

"Tangy," she remarked, smacking her lips. "I don't suppose you have any more? I suppose such delicacies are hard to come by?"

"If you'll move the lake, I'll give you lots of delicacies."

"I'll work for you," said the frog. "Only you mustn't let the Firebrat melt me."

"If you don't move the lake, he's going to melt both of us."

"I can swallow the lake," said the frog, "but when I've

done that, I'm simply too full to move. Have you got a chariot? The Firebrat had such a nice chariot. It had a whistle and a bell. A pity he let it go to rust and ruin."

"The fire engine!" exclaimed Sean. "I forgot about the fire engine."

"I know nothing about a fire engine," said the frog. "And I haven't seen the chariot for ages."

"Do you think the fire en— I mean, the chariot could carry us?" asked Sean.

"It could carry the whole lake if it had a mind to," said the frog. "The chariot has lots of places for carrying things."

"Can we trust it?" said Sean. "It's made out of knives and lost tempers, and it's mean."

"Tell the chariot you'll make it a hero. Promise you'll give it a medal."

"But I haven't got a medal."

"Surely a magician who draws delicacies out of thin air can make a medal. I'll call the chariot, the way the Firebrat did."

And the frog put two webbed fingers into her mouth and whistled a long, thin *wheeeeee*!

On the other side of the lake, something came crashing through the underbrush. Gleaming on the shore like a brass band stood the fire engine.

"Excuse me," said the frog to Sean. "Let me handle this."

Into the lake she sprang. Sean watched her skim just under the surface, growing smaller and smaller, till she was lost to sight, and he wanted to kick himself.

"Why did I let her go?" he muttered. "Now I can never help Molly. How could I have been so stupid?"

"Granddaughter of the Honorable Edna," said the snake, "if you're ready, I'll show you your road."

"Wait," said Molly. "Tell me how to charm the giant salamanders."

"Can't," said the snake. "I can only tell you their heart's desire. You'll have to work out the charm for yourself."

Molly's stomach fluttered.

"Wh—what is their heart's desire?"

"They're bored," said the snake. "They've been guarding the Firebrat's heart for years with no one to talk to but each other."

The snake nosed the space under the ruby throne.

"Your road leads to the bottom of the Lake of Fire. Granddaughter of the Honorable Edna, follow me."

The snake glided through the opening and disappeared.

"Wait for me!"

The instant Molly set foot in the passage, the stones rumbled and scraped and shut fast behind her. The snake had vanished, and the hall in which she found herself was much higher than it had looked from the outside. The floor was polished jet and the walls a mass of smoky diamonds, lit by torches that flickered behind them.

Thump!

Thump!

Thump!

She glanced around but couldn't see the deathdrum. Perhaps nobody ever sees it, she thought.

And she started to run.

In the wall ahead of her—for the hall turned sharply to the left—she saw herself sprawling on the slick floor, and behind the image of herself, the flames silently applauded.

"I want to go home!" she wailed, and she rubbed the rattlesnake ring.

And the girl in the glass wailed too.

The flames parted like curtains, and now the girl in the glass was sitting on a bed, Molly's bed in her own room at home, and her father was standing in the doorway. Their lips were moving, and though Molly could not hear the words, she knew them by heart:

It will only be for a month, Molly.

Why me? Why not Betty? She's older.

Because I think you'll do a better job than Betty. You're the reader in this family. The storyteller.

"Thank you, dear snake," said Molly, and caught her breath.

Thump!

Thump!

Thump!

Behind the glass, behind the image of herself and her father, she saw the Firebrat. He was whipping Killkeep on—fast! faster!—and the Red Crow flew before him and the ragged beasts of the fire sprang after him, but they were still far away, as small as a ship in a bottle.

Molly scrambled to her feet. This time she did not slip, but when the passage took another sharp turn, she was running so fast she nearly crashed into the wall.

Around the corner the passage ended. Before her rose a flight of black marble stairs. On the top step loomed a black marble coffin; the twelve giant salamanders were wrapping themselves around it, watching her. As she put her foot on the first step, they blazed into a fence of living flames.

On the third step, she sat down.

"I—I've come to tell you a story," she began weakly.

The salamanders turned on her their unblinking stare.

"I come from a long line of storytellers," she went on. She could hear herself babbling, her words tumbling out faster and faster. "My grandmother is a storyteller, and my father is a storyteller. Seems like my father is always picking up the phone and hearing how this kid or that kid wants me to come over because I tell such great stories."

"Begin," said the salamanders.

"Once upon a time," she squeaked. Her voice sounded so small and shaky that she hardly recognized it herself. The flames died down, but the salamanders glowed like embers.

"Once upon a time there were twelve giant salamanders who—who had an adventure."

Thump!

Thump!

Thump!

The salamanders leaned forward.

"A story about us?" hissed one.

Molly nodded. She could not help it: she was trembling all over.

"Can you tell us a story of love and honor?" crackled another.

She nodded again. Her mouth felt too dry to speak.

"With water in it? And weather?" added a third.

"Oh, lots of water and weather," said Molly.

Thump!

Thump!

Thump!

The salamanders murmured among themselves for a few minutes before they howled, "Come up where we can hear you! Come up where we can hear you!"

"Do you promise not to turn me to ashes?"

"We promise!" cried all the salamanders together.

She took a deep breath and ran up the marble steps and sat down among the salamanders, who gathered in a shimmering knot at her feet.

"You can all be in the story," she said, "if you'll open this coffin for me."

"We can't open the coffin," said the salamanders. "Only the heart inside can open it. Tell us your story. Maybe the heart will listen."

Thump!

Thump!

Thump!

"Once there were twelve salamanders who lived in a forest full of—of weather. It rained every day."

The salamanders lifted their heads.

"The forest was also full of treasure. After the rain, the salamanders would go out to see what the rain had brought them. Such wonderful things it brought them! An apple—"

She reached into her pocket and took out the neverhunger apple.

"What's that?" asked the salamanders.

"An apple," said Molly.

"And what do you do with it?"

"You share it," she said.

"What's *share*?" asked the smallest salamander.

"Each of you gets a piece," said Molly. She unfastened her barrette, and using the metal clasp, she cut the apple

into twelve pieces, which she passed to the salamanders. All the salamanders began to clamor at once.

"Let me try it, let me try it!"

"There's a piece for each of you," said Molly, eying the closed coffin. She wiped the barrette on her sleeve and put it back in her hair. Behind the smacking of lips Molly heard the warning of the deathdrum.

Thump!

Thump!

Thump!

"Get on with the story," said the biggest salamander.

What was that other noise, that high whine? Behind the glass the Firebrat was galloping toward her and sharpening his feelers on his sword. The lid of the coffin had not moved. Terror swept over her, and when she tried to speak, she could hardly find her voice.

"A big storm came. The water made a river through the forest. And when the storm was over, what do you think the salamanders found, shining in a gully? A heart of gold. And one of the salamanders said, 'Let's leave it for the girl who saved our cousin, the king of the snakes, from the Dog.' 'Yes, let's,' said the other salamanders. So they left it out where she would be sure to find it. The first time she came to the forest, she didn't find the heart."

With a sigh, the hinges of the coffin adjusted themselves, and the lid trembled and lifted ever so little. Molly could see the Firebrat plainly now, and she could no longer keep her voice steady.

"The second time she came to the forest, she didn't find the heart."

The lid lifted higher, a hair's breadth.

"But the third time, she found the heart. And since it was her grandmother's birthday, she said to herself, 'I'll give her this heart for a present.' "

"What's a birthday?" asked the smallest salamander. "Is it the beginning of the story?"

"It—it's like a story," whispered Molly.

"What's a present?" asked another salamander.

"It's what you give to a person you love," said Molly.

The Firebrat was bounding over the flames. In another minute he would be among them.

"Ah, it's a kind of story," said a third salamander. "We understand. Go on."

Again the hinges sighed, and like an eye opening, the lid lifted enough to admit a gleam of light.

"So the girl polished the heart and wrapped it in tissue and brought it to her grandmother on the morning of her birthday. When her grandmother opened the heart, she started to cry. 'Where on earth did you find this?' she exclaimed. 'In the woods,' said the girl. And the grandmother said, 'A boy I liked gave me this when I was in sixth grade, and I lost it.' Then the grandmother opened the heart, and what do you think she found?"

At these words the lid of the coffin flew all the way open.

"She found a paper that said YOU HAVE WON MY HEART."

The Firebrat's heart skipped out of the coffin, and Molly snatched it just as Killkeep slashed through the wall.

"My heart," hissed the Firebrat. "Give it to me."

By the light of his eyes, which struck sparks as he rolled them, she saw Killkeep glowing, first red-hot, then white-hot.

"Give him his heart," sighed the salamanders.

"Not until you give me the timesticks," said Molly.

Killkeep tapped Molly's left foot, and she felt nothing but the cold weight of iron, for iron it had become. The armor hadn't helped; she felt as if the whole world had betrayed her.

"Give up his heart," said the salamanders.

Like a flaming paintbrush, Killkeep drew a door in the air, sketched in fire.

"Do you see that door?" asked the Firebrat. "That will take you back to your own country. Give me back my heart, and I'll give you back your foot and send you home."

"My friend, too?"

"Your friend, too."

The door swayed open, and Molly could see her grandmother asleep in her chair, holding the box of snapshots on her lap. The door opened a little wider, and the scene changed to the shop, and there was the table, its three chairs drawn up. On the table someone had left a plate of onion rolls and a bowl of apples, as if Molly and Sean were expected.

The flames on the timesticks trembled.

"Give me the timesticks," said Molly.

A tap on her right foot numbed it. When Killkeep struck it—*clang!*—she felt nothing; she had a gleaming foot of copper. The Red Crow swooped past her head and gave a long sizzling cry.

"Give me my heart, and I'll give you your feet. You may as well give up. When Killkeep touches your hand, you'll drop my heart, and I shall change you into a little firebrat and whip you with knives of fire when you don't mind me."

"If I drop your heart, it will break," whispered Molly.

Tap. Her left hand twinkled to silver.

"You'll drop it and I'll catch it," sneered the Firebrat. "I'll use your silver arms to hang my swords on."

Killkeep lunged for her right hand.

I'm lost, thought Molly.

A tremendous crash behind her sent Killkeep flying, and through the wall burst the fire engine shouting "Fire!" and Sean yelling "Let out the lake! Now! Now!"

Molly was terrified. Over the roar of falling water, the fire engine could be heard singing:

> *"Water leaps as if delighted,*
> *While her conquered foes retire,*
> *Round the aqueducts of glory*
> *With the baffled demon fire!"*

Such a howling and sizzling and steaming! Rocks split like peals of thunder, smoke blackened the air, the fire engine went up in smoke; indeed, everything around Molly was turning to steam, which hissed and swirled around Sean.

The Lake of Fire was gone, leaving in its wake the singing of many streams. Molly felt a warmth rushing first into her left hand and then into her feet, and she knew they were iron and copper and silver no longer. Around her, moss and forget-me-nots and wild thyme were growing out of the ashes. Just overhead hovered a crystal palace. Pagodas glimmered over roses of silver and jade, silver staircases wound among terraced gardens, sapphire dragonflies and emerald birds darted to and fro while men and women in shimmering robes strolled and laughed under the crystal trees.

In a cloak of roses and pearls a radiant child was skipping around the wicker arbor and trying to keep his crown from slipping. Moonstones and diamonds scattered circles of light over him, and the torn Dracula mask swung from his arm as if it were nodding at Molly and Sean.

"Sean, Sean, what's happening?" cried Molly. "Where's the Firebrat?"

"I don't know, but oh, Molly, look!"

Striding toward them was a tall, dazzling figure that glowed like a crystal as he lifted his golden hands to greet Sean and Molly, who ran toward him, shouting, "Eugene!"

"To the great magicians who saved the timesticks," said Eugene, "all the crystal people give thanks. And for freeing me from the Firebrat's spell—"

"For giving us back our wise magician," crowed the radiant child, taking Eugene by the hand, "I, the Perfect Emperor, give thanks."

Molly and Sean gazed around them in astonishment. The beeches and sycamores and oaks had turned to trees of pure crystal. Leaf rang on leaf, birds feathered in emeralds darted to and fro, dragonflies hummed and thrummed. Here was the garden, just as Molly had imagined it, the crystal ferns bowing, the crystal roses sparkling, the boughs of crystal apples and pears chiming against each other like far-off bells.

The radiant child bowed first to Molly and then to Sean and threw his Dracula mask into the air.

"We're free! The timesticks are safe!"

"The timesticks—where are the timesticks?" asked Sean.

"Not sticks anymore, but stars," said Eugene. "Don't you see them rising over the roof of the palace? They'll stay lit forever. And their last act will be to carry us home. While I'm gone, keep an eye on things, won't you?"

And he slipped off his ring and gave it to Sean. The eye regarded Sean with great interest. Then it winked at him.

"You've brought us back to ourselves," said the child. "Please don't go. I, the Perfect Emperor, invite you to stay with us forever."

Molly felt a sudden longing to watch TV with Grandma, to rummage through Grandma's box of old snapshots, to hunt for treasures in Grandma's shop.

"Where are we?" she asked. She was almost afraid to ask.

"You are not far from home," answered Eugene. "And neither are we. Since we could not go to our island, our island has come for us."

"It's a marvelous place," said the Perfect Emperor. "You'll love it."

"I think I'd rather go home," said Sean. He could not explain why, even to himself, but he was sure it had something to do with the onion rolls his mother bought on her way home from work and with the happiness that filled him when he heard her key click in the lock.

"Can you show us the way back?" asked Molly.

"The way you came is now the way back," said Eugene. "Rap your golden fish against the arbor. But before you go, Molly, don't forget your heart."

"You mean the Firebrat's heart?" said Molly. "No, thanks."

"Magic changes things," said Eugene.

He stooped and pushed aside the moss at her feet and lifted up a little golden heart and slipped it into her hand. How warm it felt, and how smooth.

"Oh, I forgot the fire engine!" exclaimed Sean. "Where is the fire engine? I promised it a medal."

Eugene laughed. "Keep your eyes open for that fire engine. You never know where things will turn up."

Under the crystal trees a band struck up a lively tune.

"I hope we meet again," said the Perfect Emperor. "If you ever find yourself on the Sea of Forgetfulness, you are always welcome on our island."

"I wish the tortoise was here," said Molly.

"When you destroyed the Firebrat, you broke the power of all who worked harm in his kingdom. Keep a lookout for that tortoise," said Eugene. "Are you ready?"

Sean clicked his golden fish against the arbor and stepped through, but Molly hesitated.

"Thank you, Eugene," she said. "For everything."

She clicked her fish once, twice, three times. As she followed Sean through the arbor, she heard Eugene call after them, "My magic is Loving Care, my dear, Loving Care."

The ground was shaking under their feet. Far away a

train rumbled closer and closer. The sound faded as brightness fell from the air, and everything grew dark.

Now they heard the familiar racket of traffic, the taxis honking, the buses rumbling.

When the dark lifted, they found themselves on the other side of the locked gate. Sean's flashlight lay on the steps, shining its thin beam through the branches of the dead Christmas tree. There was the park, with its tide of trash and its sad pigeons and wooden benches. The four men in hard hats had just finished their lunch.

Suddenly they caught themselves listening attentively to a dry, scraping sound on the pavement, a familiar huffing and puffing.

An old, old man in a worn green overcoat was peering down at them.

"We—we're looking for the subway," faltered Sean.

"This station is closed, children. I could have directed you to the nearest station if you'd asked me, but it's too late now. You've gotten yourselves all dirty. I see you've torn your shirt sleeve, miss. And you've got a nasty scratch on your cheek, sir."

He reached into his coat pocket and pulled out a safety pin, which he handed to Molly, and a Band-Aid, which he gave to Sean, and started to shuffle away.

All at once he changed his mind and turned back.

"Do you have the fare to get home?" he asked, and without waiting for their reply, he gave each of them a shiny subway token and an apple.

Never had daylight felt so friendly, never had roaring traffic, whining sirens, blaring radios, screeching brakes, and crowds of folks jostling to and fro under the afternoon sun made such a joyful noise to their ears as when Molly and Sean turned the corner and crossed the street to the shop: THE SILVER SHUTTLE: OLD AND NEW, NEAR AND FAR.

The door stood open. Who was that moving about in the shop? Grandma?

"I'm cleaning up," she called out. "Where have you been? You can't imagine what good luck I've had." She was rubbing a wet rag over the chairs around the table, which was set with a plate of onion rolls and a bowl of apples.

As they stepped into the shop they heard the tinkle of a music box: the golden bird was singing in its cage.

"Grandma, I'm so glad to see you!" exclaimed Molly. "And look what I found!"

And she gave her grandmother the little golden heart. Grandma studied it appraisingly.

"It's for you," added Molly.

"Isn't that pretty?" said Grandma. She looked genuinely pleased. "It would look lovely on a golden chain. I came down to the shop looking for you two, and I found a strand of pearls that Eugene had left. Cultured pearls."

She pointed to a strand of pearls around her neck.

"They were all tangled up with a Medal of Courage from the Staatsburg Volunteer Fire Department. Somebody worked hard for that medal. Sean, would you like it? It's dated 1881. I put it in the case. Go have a look at it."

Sean took the medal from the case and walked over to the little toy fire engine. "I think it looks good right here," he said as he hung the medal on the front fender.

"But here comes the best part," said Grandma. "At the bottom of the box I found the ugliest ceramic frog you've ever seen. Stamped on the bottom was 'Souvenir of Frog Hollow, Vermont.' Frog Hollow! That's where Cora Dibble lives. I'd lost track of her for years—lost the name of the town. And here it was, right in my own shop."

"Who's Cora Dibble?" asked Molly.

"How could you forget?" said Grandma. "She's the girl in the picture I showed you. We're holding a big snake, remember?"

"I remember the snake," said Molly slowly. "I don't think I'll ever forget that snake."

"I got her number through information and called her," said Grandma. "It was wonderful talking to her again. She's going to visit me next time she's in New York. Have an onion roll. Sean, your mom brought them over. She got off work early."

"She did?" said Sean.

"She brought enough for all of us," said Grandma.

She drew Eugene's chair to the table and sat down. Molly and Sean drew up chairs on either side of her and helped themselves to the rolls.

"Imagine, finding a friend through a frog," exclaimed Grandma. "Oh, Molly, what a story that would make!"

NANCY WILLARD has written many award-winning books for children and young adults, ranging from her brilliant book of poems *A Visit to William Blake's Inn*, which was awarded the 1982 Newbery Medal, to her novel *Things Invisible to See*, which was honored as a Young Adult Best Book by the American Library Association. Ms. Willard's inspiration for *Firebrat* came from a poster David Wiesner originally illustrated for an art exhibit and on which he based the jacket painting for this book. She is a lecturer at Vassar College and an instructor at the Bread Loaf Writers' Conference, and lives in Poughkeepsie, New York, with her husband and son.

DAVID WIESNER graduated from the Rhode Island School of Design and has illustrated five books for children, most recently the highly praised *The Loathsome Dragon*, which he wrote in collaboration with his wife, Kim Kahng. They live in Brooklyn, New York.